The JN-4D circled the field and came swooping down low over the crowd. Lizzie's hair fluttered in the back draft, and she gave a loud whoop.

The Jenny climbed high and steep. Up, up, up. Lizzie held her breath as the aeroplane went over and flew on its back before looping back around to the upright position. She finally exhaled.

Next he rolled the aeroplane sideways several times. She cheered right along with the crowd as he passed over. Then the Jenny climbed high into the air, turned, and came back down.

He started spinning out of control. Around and around.

Gasps came from the crowd. Lizzie couldn't breathe and held the dog tight to her chest. Her heart beat faster and faster as the yellow aeroplane raced, spinning toward the ground. He was going to crash.

"No!"

Women in the crowd screamed.

Just then, he pulled out of it and waved to the crowd as he flew over. Lizzie stared for a moment, comprehending what had just happened, then set the dog down and jumped to her feet, applauding. She wanted to do that.

Pete landed again, jumped down, and swooped off his helmet. "Who wants to take the first ride? I promise to keep your ride smooth and level. No stunts with passengers onboard."

Lizzie stared at the man who'd taken her breath away and made her heart race with his aerial stunts. She wanted to push her way through the dozen-and-a-half or so people and beg to be the first, but she wanted more from this flyboy than just a ride. So much more. She would just have to wait. When he'd garnered his wages from everyone else, he'd be more amiable to her request.

MARY DAVIS is a full-time writer whose first published novel was *Newlywed Games* from Multnomah. She enjoys going into schools and talking to kids about writing. Mary lives near Colorado's Rocky Mountains with her husband, three teens, and seven pets. Please visit her Web site at marydavisbooks.com.

Books by Mary Davis

HEARTSONG PRESENTS

Don't miss out on any of our super romances. Write to us at the following address for information on our newest releases and club information.

Heartsong Presents Readers' Service
PO Box 721
Uhrichsville, OH 44683

Or visit www.heartsongpresents.com

Reckless Rogue

Mary Davis

Heartsong Presents

To Grandma Elizabeth Calkin
And to Pete

A note from the Author:
I love to hear from my readers! You may correspond with me by writing:

Mary Davis
Author Relations
PO Box 721
Uhrichsville, OH 44683

ISBN 978-1-60260-047-8

RECKLESS ROGUE

All scripture quotations are taken from the King James Version of the Bible.

All of the characters and events in this book are fictitious. Any resemblance to actual persons, living or dead, or to actual events is purely coincidental.

Our mission is to publish and distribute inspirational products offering exceptional value and biblical encouragement to the masses.

PRINTED IN THE U.S.A.

one

Washington, 1920

Lizzie Carter shaded her goggle-covered eyes with her hand as she looked toward the blue sky. A yellow bi-plane flew overhead. It sent her heart racing. To be free of gravity that held her to the ground and free of injustice toward women. One day she would fly, too.

"Lizzie, look out!" her twelve-year-old brother, Ivan, yelled from the passenger seat of the Ford Model T.

She turned her attention back to the winding dirt road leading from town to their small farm and saw the maple tree coming straight toward her. She slammed her feet on the brake and clutch as she cranked the wheel to the left and skidded just past the huge trunk. Her right tire plunked into a rut and hissed out all its air.

She shoved her goggles up and got out to survey the damage. "Well, isn't this a fine pickle."

Ivan got out and removed the jack, then began loosening the bolts that held the spare tire on. "Hurry up, Lizzie. I want to see where he lands." Ivan kept one eye on the sky as he worked.

She was just as eager not to lose sight of the aerial pheno-menon. Never did she expect an aeroplane to be flying over her small town of Cashmere. She shaded her eyes. The bi-plane was but a spot on the far end of town. There was no way to catch him. She kicked the dusty road. There was no hurry now.

Ivan had the car jacked up, and she removed the flat tire

as Ivan lifted the spare into place. She tossed the tire on the floor of the backseat. When Ivan finished and turned toward the empty blue sky, he looked as disappointed and dejected as she felt. He slammed the automobile door after he got in, but it bounced back open. Three times. He jumped out and pushed the door closed. "I'll just walk home."

"Get in. We'll drop this tire off at the station to be repaired and head in the direction he was flying. I'll drive all the way to Wenatchee if I have to. He likely landed there. He probably needs gasoline. Someone oughtta know where he went or if he landed." Lizzie opened the throttle, pressed the clutch, and pushed the starter button. The Ford rumbled to life, and she lowered her goggles into place.

Ivan crawled in through the open window and tumbled into the passenger seat, struggling to right his lanky body.

"I guess you don't care about fishing anymore?" Ivan had talked her into taking him up Tumwater Canyon to fish.

She eased the clutch back into slow speed, and when they were going fast enough, allowed the pedal all the way up into high speed and partially closed the throttle. They were off toward town to find that aeroplane.

She pulled into the gasoline station, shut off the engine, and jumped out while Ivan remained slumped in the front seat.

"Hi, Bill." She waved at the aging station owner who came out immediately.

"Hello, darlin'. I filled up the gasoline tank on your Tin Lizzie not more than twenty minutes ago, so you must have come back for my charmin' good looks." Bill gave her a gummy grin.

She smiled back at the friendly old-timer. "Where are your teeth?"

"They was hurtin' me so I spit them out. I was about to paste them back in when you pulled up again. If I put them back in, will you give me a kiss?" Bill puckered his already puckery lips.

She shook her head. "I blew a tire on these stupid rutted roads. Can you fix it for me?" She pulled it out of the back.

Bill took the tire and set it on the ground in front of him. "Shoot, Lizzie, you know I can fix anythin'."

"Thanks, Bill." She gave him a peck on his leathery old cheek.

Bill let out a hiss that was supposed to be a whistle, then hopped around on one foot. "Lizzie kissed me, Lizzie kissed me."

She had to smile. She'd made an old man happy. "I'll come back later for the tire."

"It'll be ready." Bill had a spring in his step as he rolled the tire into the garage.

Lizzie climbed back into the black Model T, opened the throttle, and pressed the electric start. "I'm going to stop by the post office and tell Daddy about the tire." Daddy didn't drive because of his false leg, but he wanted to know everything that happened with "the heap of scrap metal he paid good money for." Daddy hated all automobiles; thought they were from the devil or something. But missing a leg and not being able to walk to town had softened him to the idea of having one even if he didn't like it. Daddy had depended on her for everything since Mom died seven years ago.

Ivan's eyes widened. "You aren't going to tell him about going to Wenatchee and looking for the aeroplane, are you?"

Did her brother truly think she was that stupid? Was it because she was a girl? Or was he looking after his own hide? "Daddy's let me drive to Wenatchee before."

"With him in the front seat with you."

"He never said I couldn't go. And who's going to tell him, anyway?"

Ivan pressed his lips tight and shook his head.

She motored two blocks over and parked in front of the

post office. "I'll be right back."

Ivan crossed his arms and slunk lower in the leather seat.

She went inside and waited as her dad hobbled his way over to the mailboxes and retrieved mail for Mrs. Stevens. His peg leg thumped on the wooden floor. "Here you go, Mertle."

Lizzie went over to her dad when he was through. "Have a seat."

"Too much work to do." He smiled at her. "But I'm always glad to see my beautiful Elizabeth." Her dad refused to use her preferred nickname. He said Elizabeth was a good sensible name. Lizzie was for flappers and floozies. "I thought you'd gone home."

"We were on our way when one of the tires went flat. We dropped it off at Bill's Garage. I just came to let you know and see if you need anything."

"Nope. I'm fine."

The automobile's horn started a wild beat. She looked out the window and saw Ivan get out and wave his arms frantically to her.

Daddy peered toward the window. "What's his problem? Sometimes I wonder if he's touched in the head."

Ivan pointed toward the sky.

"Oh, he's just fussing to go." She scooted toward the door as she spoke. "He's sore at me for making him change the flat. I promised him I wouldn't be long. I'll be back at closing. Love you, Daddy." She slipped outside and held the door open for slim Mrs. Baker and her three-year-old son.

Ivan grabbed her by the arm and pulled her toward the car. "Hurry. He's back. He's flying toward the west side of town. I bet he's going to land in that old field of Mr. Johnson's."

Lizzie jumped in and pressed the electric start. The engine choked. Then she remembered to open the throttle. She was sure glad she'd talked Daddy into the new electric-start model when they bought it last January. It was a whole lot easier on the body than the old crank models. No sprained wrists or broken bones.

She didn't want any trouble, so she kept to a leisurely pace as she headed back the way they'd come until she got to the edge of town, then pushed the automobile as hard as she dared on the rutted road. She couldn't afford another flat tire. She had no spare now.

❧

Lieutenant Pete Garfield touched the wheels of his Curtiss JN-4D down as softly as possible on the uneven field. It was a beautiful landing. One of his best, but he was sure his traveling companion on this short flight would find complaint in it somewhere. Old Finn had complained about everything else. Not everyone found joy in being free of God-given earth. He didn't mind. It left more open blue sky for him to trek across. There was nothing else like it. Free from everything down below. Free from condemning glares and accusations. Free to be with God on His own terms. But sadly, he was back on the ground.

He scratched the head of the little brown terrier who shared his seat. "You liked it, didn't you, Fred?"

Fred leaned back and licked his chin.

He maneuvered the aeroplane to the far end of the field and turned it around, ready for its next flight. A Model T was bouncing across the uneven ground toward him. His first customer. Small towns could sometimes be more profitable than the large ones.

He unhooked Fred from his harness and climbed out onto the wing with him. He jumped to the ground, set Fred down, then turned to help Finn.

Finn, now out on the wing with a death grip on one of the wing's tension wires, slapped his hand away. "Haven't you done enough?"

Fred barked and hopped on his back feet, trying to coax a smile from Finn by waving his front paws.

Pete stifled a laugh at Finn's gruffness. "I'm only trying to help." As long as the seventy-something-year-old man was still feisty, Pete didn't worry about him giving up on life.

Finn held out a gnarled hand. "Well, then give me a hand so I can get back on earth where I belong."

Pete thumped his palm to his forehead. "Why didn't I think of that?" Taking a firm hold of the old man's arm and wrapping his other arm around Finn's back, Pete helped ease his dear friend's thin frame to the ground. "See. Safe and sound just like I promised."

"Safe and sound! I nearly died up there." Finn pulled off the leather helmet. His white hair was in disarray, sticking up in all directions. He slapped the helmet onto the wing, pulled his crushed hat out from under his coat, and poked his fist inside before ramming it onto his head. "I'm never going up in that contraption again." He walked away.

Pete smiled at Finn's back. It had only been a short trip from Wenatchee over to Cashmere. It had taken him a long time to talk Finn into letting him fly him over. It was faster and smoother. Obviously, Finn didn't think so. He didn't like motorized "contraptions." Pete felt much safer in his aeroplane than he did in an automobile.

Finn opened the door of the Ford and tipped his hat to the doll climbing out of the driver's seat. Pete hustled over to Finn. The old man shouldn't get all the accolades from the young lady. He doffed his helmet and finger-combed his brown curls before joining Finn at the black Model T.

The lady brushed her light brown hair with red highlights back from her face. Almost a cinnamon color. He could tell a mock bob hung just below her chin. He'd seen it before. Ladies who didn't want or weren't allowed to cut their long hair into the modern bob pinned their hair back at the nape of their neck, leaving enough pulled forward to simulate a bob. It told him a lot about her. She was trying to be a modern woman, perhaps even a flapper, but wasn't quite there yet. Real flappers had no inhibitions and cut their hair whether family and friends protested or not.

He bowed. "Lieutenant Pete Garfield at your service."

She opened her mouth, but before she could speak, the boy of about twelve piped up.

"You flew in the Great War?"

He wasn't going to have to finagle his war exploits into the conversation. The boy had done it for him. He liked this boy already.

"I certainly did."

"Did you battle the Red Baron?"

"As a matter of fact, the baron and I did share the same sky once. It was a fierce dogfight. There were German Fokkers, British Sopwith Camels, French Nieuports all over the sky. It was hard to tell who were the good guys. The sky was full of smoke from the automatic guns and shot-up aeroplanes, mostly Germans." He glanced toward the doll to see if she was captivated with his exploits at war. She was staring off toward his aeroplane. Was she picturing him in that craft in the battle? He hoped so. "We were lucky not to crash into each other. I caught a glimpse of a red tri-plane Fokker and knew it was Baron Manfred von Richthofen. I banked right and got on his tail. I was just about to shoot him down when artillery fire came out of nowhere and took the Red Baron out of the sky. The rest of the Germans were so scared they turned tail and flew home to Mama as fast as they could."

Tail wagging, Fred rose up on his back paws again and waved his front ones to the boy.

The boy got down on his knees and scratched Fred behind the ears. "What's his name?"

"Fred."

"I'll see you around." Finn gave Pete a wave and strode off.

"I'll be right back," he said to the doll and quickly caught up to Finn. "You want me to walk into town with you? I bet I can get the doll and the boy to give us a ride."

"I'd like to keep my feet on solid ground. I never did like motorized contraptions. I'll be fine. I got business to attend to here." Finn always was a loner, drifting from one place to another, in and out of people's lives. And town was not more than a mile away.

He watched Finn walk off, then turned back to see the boy putting on and adjusting the helmet that Finn had left on the wing. He walked up to the boy. "You got a name, kid?"

"Ivan. Can I have a ride in your aeroplane?"

"Sure. Where's the doll you came with?"

Ivan pointed toward the front of his craft.

She stroked the nose like a favored pet. No doubt dreaming of the pilot who flew her.

"What's her name?" The two looked alike, and he guessed brother and sister.

"Lizzie."

"She's your sister, right?"

The boy nodded.

"Thanks. Um, don't go climbing around on this until I tell you it's okay." He patted the side of his aeroplane, then strode around the other side and peeked around the nose at the doll. His heart stirred. This was the one. He always picked one girl in every crowd that he'd steal a kiss from before he flew off to a new place. Even though the crowd so far only consisted of her and her brother, he knew she was special, and he wanted a kiss from her. "Hi, Lizzie."

She sucked in a breath as she looked up at him. "How did. . . ? Never mind. Ivan." She turned back to his aeroplane.

"Her name is Jenny."

"The nickname for the Curtiss JN-4D."

"That's right." He was impressed she knew that and was about to impress her with his knowledge when she went on.

"Does it have the standard ninety horsepower OX5 engine?"

He stared openmouthed at her. Most men didn't know the specs of his craft. How could a doll? He nodded dumbly, then managed to say, "I painted it yellow."

"Yellow looks good on her." Lizzie never took her eyes off the Jenny and slowly walked the length.

Her close scrutiny of his craft made him a little uneasy. What was she looking for? Did she know more than just rote memory specs?

"In the Great War, I flew a British Sopwith Camel with a synchronized Vickers gun firing through the propeller and a rear-mounted Lewis." She didn't seem interested so he added, "I normally charge five bucks for a ride around the sky, but for you, Lizzie, I'll do it for free." That ought to give her a thrill and get him a kiss. But she didn't even glance his direction.

"Can I have a free ride, too?" Ivan had come from somewhere and broken the connection Pete was trying to form with Lizzie.

"If you fetch my gasoline for the day, I'll give you an extralong ride."

Ivan slapped his thigh. "Hot dog."

Three more cars rolled onto the field. "Time for this flyboy to go to work." He winked at Lizzie, who'd finally looked up at him, then walked over to the growing crowd that would become his paying customers. People were fascinated with aeroplanes and would pay for a ride, and he was just the man to relieve them of their money and give them an adventure they would never forget.

two

Lizzie watched the lieutenant taxi his Curtiss JN-4D down the bumpy field. He found a smooth strip and pushed the throttle. The engine roared, and the Jenny took off down the field, then up into the air. Lizzie sucked in a breath, and Fred barked at his master leaving him behind. She felt the same. What it must feel like at that first moment when you knew you had left earth. You knew you were free.

The JN-4D circled the field and came swooping down low over the crowd. Lizzie's hair fluttered in the back draft, and she gave a loud whoop. The Jenny climbed high and steep. Up, up, up. Lizzie held her breath as the aeroplane went over and flew on its back before looping back around to the upright position. She finally exhaled.

Next he rolled the aeroplane sideways several times. She cheered right along with the crowd as he passed over. Then the Jenny climbed high into the air, turned, and came back down.

He started spinning out of control. Around and around.

Gasps came from the crowd. Lizzie couldn't breathe and held the dog tight to her chest. Her heart beat faster and faster as the yellow aeroplane raced, spinning toward the ground. He was going to crash.

"No!"

Women in the crowd screamed.

Just then, he pulled out of it and waved to the crowd as he flew over. Lizzie stared for a moment, comprehending what had just happened, then set the dog down and jumped to her feet, applauding. She wanted to do that.

Pete landed again, jumped down, and swooped off his helmet. "Who wants to take the first ride? I promise to keep your ride smooth and level. No stunts with passengers onboard."

Lizzie stared at the man who'd taken her breath away and made her heart race with his aerial stunts. She wanted to push her way through the dozen-and-a-half or so people and beg to be the first, but she wanted more from this flyboy than just a ride. So much more. She would just have to wait. When he'd garnered his wages from everyone else, he'd be more amiable to her request.

Pete excused himself from the crowd and came over to her with Ivan at his side, carrying a portable gasoline tank. "The kid said you'd ferry him back and forth from the gasoline station."

"Sure." She opened the back door of the Model T for her brother, who started to set the tank on the seat. "Put it on the floor, silly." Ivan complied, moving his fishing pole out of the way.

Pete gave some money to cover the fuel and went back to his waiting audience, and she and Ivan motored off to town. She didn't want to leave. She wanted to watch each and every time that beautiful piece of machinery took off and landed. She wanted the image carved deep into her memory so she could play it over and over when this flyboy left for greener pastures. She pulled into Bill's Garage.

Bill came out of the weatherworn wooden building, wiping his greasy hands on a greasy rag. In fact, most of Bill's attire was permanently grease stained. "I just got your tire fixed." His words were a bit muffled between his gums.

"Swell. I need this extra tank filled with gasoline."

Bill squinted at the tank Ivan was taking out of the back. "Whose is it?"

"The flyboy's. Did you see the yellow aeroplane fly overhead?"

"Who could miss it? You think if I put in my teeth, he'll

take me up in his aeroplane?"

"Of course. He's offering rides for five dollars apiece."

"You don't let him leave before I get there."

"Ivan here volunteered to fetch his gasoline, and guess who's stuck helping him?" She tried to sound put out.

"You're about as disappointed as an ant colony when a sandwich gets dropped on top of their hill."

She broke into a wide smile. "I'm going to get to fly. I never believed this would actually happen. Who would think a real live pilot would land in little ole Cashmere?"

"I guess it's better than a dead pilot." Bill winked at her.

She shook her head at his humor. "Don't tell my dad."

"If I haven't told him about that half-built contraption you got out back of my shed, why would I tell him about this? But I think he might figure you saw it when word gets around town."

"Speaking of that, tell everyone who stops in to come out to Johnson's field for aeroplane rides." She wanted this flyboy to hang around for the entire day. She paid Bill for the tire and for the gasoline Ivan pumped.

The day passed with Lizzie and Ivan replenishing the fuel and the lieutenant taking person after person up. Bill had come out and gone for three rides. The lieutenant only let him pay for the first one, so Bill gave him some free gasoline. At the end of the day, the flyboy had to send several people away with the promise of another chance tomorrow.

Dorcas, Agnes, and Margaret, three girls from town whom Lizzie had gone to school with, fawned over Pete all day, smiling and flirting in their bobbed hair and knee-length dresses. The lieutenant lapped up every bit of attention the ladies dished out, before and after he'd given them rides. All three promised to return the next day.

The sun was dipping toward the mountains, and Ivan was up in the air. As promised, his ride was longer than the others.

Lizzie would be the last passenger for today, but her trip up would be different.

ॐ

Pete turned his Jenny around, pointing it into the wind, ready for his next and last passenger for the day. And the one he looked forward to the most. This small town had been more profitable than he'd expected. He hadn't thought he'd have enough passengers to fill the day, and he had people coming back tomorrow. He hoped Lizzie would be back. He'd hardly gotten to see her at all. Half the time when he landed, she was off retrieving his fuel, which he was very grateful for; the other half, she stayed at a distance with Fred curled up in her lap. Lucky dog. She did bring him lunch but wasn't around to eat with him. Ivan was. He was a good kid, but Pete would rather spend his time with a beautiful doll.

Now it would be Lizzie's turn, and he wouldn't be able to talk to her up in the air, only look at the back of her head.

Ivan jumped out and to the ground, swiping off the helmet like he was born doing it. "Hot dog, that was fun." He handed the helmet to Lizzie. "You're going to love it."

Pete hoped she would. Enough to return tomorrow. He went over to her and took the ends of the helmet strap from her hands. She'd been doing fine, but he wanted to help, so he buckled the helmet securely on her head. "I'm just going to fill the tank. You can climb on up." He held her hand, helping her up onto the wing, then turned to fill the tank.

"Hey, Ivan. Do you think you can talk your sister into coming back tomorrow? Tell her I need you to fetch gasoline for me again."

"Ask me something hard. She'd be glad to do it."

"Are you sure?"

"When we first saw you fly overhead, she ran off the road and nearly hit a tree because she was looking up instead of at the road."

So he mesmerized little Miss Lizzie who hardly looked at him. She must be a little shy. That just made garnering a kiss a little more challenging. Tomorrow. He wouldn't push it today.

He filled the tank, then grabbed hold of a support pole and swung up onto the wing. He stopped short. Lizzie was in the back seat of the fuselage. His seat. He put on his most charming smile and leaned over the edge of the opening. "Doll, haven't you noticed all day that this is where I sit?"

She looked up at him with an impish smile and batted her eyelashes. "Mm-hm."

She was cute. There was no doubt about that. Did she think she was going to sit on his lap or something? As appealing as that was, he wouldn't be able to fly that way. "You're going to have to move up to the other seat."

"I like this one."

"I can't fly from the front seat, so if you want a ride, you'll have to move." He cocked his head toward the front.

"I'll fly."

His smile fell immediately away, and he coughed. She couldn't be serious. "What! No one flies Jenny but me."

She turned and folded her hands together. "I know I could fly her. Please let me try. I think your aeroplane is real darb."

She was trying to charm him with sweet talk and compliments. He wasn't going to bite. He was the king of schmoozing. He shook his head. He didn't want her accidentally taking off. "You don't know the first thing about piloting an aeroplane."

She pointed to the instruments one by one. "This one is the water temperature indicator, the altimeter, airspeed, oil pressure gauge, and the tach." She smiled up at him proudly.

"Impressive, but no. You either move up front or you don't get a ride at all."

&

Lizzie sized up her opponent. Would the lieutenant buckle if she pushed? If she batted her eyelashes a little more? She wanted to fly his aeroplane so badly. A ride would be fine, but she wanted to be in control. If she turned down a ride today, would he offer her another one tomorrow? She couldn't risk it. This might be her only chance ever to go up into the air. But she would give piloting one more shot. "I'm a fast learner. I bet a smart fellow like you could teach me."

He folded his arms and shook his head. "Like I said, no one but me flies her."

She stuck out her bottom lip in a feigned pout as she climbed from the pilot's seat to the other, careful to keep her mid-calf-length dress from riding up above her knee.

The flyboy settled into the seat behind her, then maneuvered the aeroplane around. "You ready?" he hollered over the engine noise.

She gave him a thumbs-up, then pretended she was actually flying.

They moved slowly at first. Then as the aeroplane sped up, the air seemed to be sucked from her lungs as they went faster and faster until the moment she felt the rough ground fall away. All was smooth. She sucked in a great breath and gripped the side of the opening. Her body pressed into the hard seat. She looked over the side as the ground pulled away from them or rather they pulled away from the ground. Free at last. She just had to be able to fly this amazing craft.

She felt a hand on her shoulder.

"It's all right. You're safe," the lieutenant yelled over the engine and wind noise.

She threw her hands straight up. "Yippee! I'm flying."

The lieutenant flew level, then circled the field. She wished he'd do one of those loops or rolls he'd done when he flew alone. She turned around and drew a circle with her finger. The lieutenant shook his head. She nodded hers. He shook his again, and she turned back around. Then he started flying higher and higher. Was he going to do a loop, after all?

Instead, he banked hard and dove toward the ground, leveling off before they were too close. She supposed he didn't want to scare her. He'd thrilled her, though. She wanted to do it again. She wanted to fly it. She pulled the bobby pins from her hair and let it fly in the wind from under the helmet.

The flight was over all too soon.

The lieutenant circled around like he'd done for all the others and lined up his craft with the field. She wanted to beg him to stay in the air but didn't. Disappointment weighed heavy when the wheels grabbed hold of the earth once again. Maybe she could finagle another ride tomorrow. Maybe she'd get him to let her fly it.

The lieutenant stopped the aeroplane and climbed out onto the wing, holding a hand out to her. She took it and stepped onto the wing with him. He jumped down, put his hands on her waist, and lowered her to the ground. That was when she looked into his chocolate brown eyes and stayed there a moment with her hands still resting on his shoulders.

"Did you like the ride?"

She removed her hands and smoothed her dress. "It was delightful."

He raised an eyebrow. "Delightful?"

"It was hardly spectacular. Your aeroplane can do far more." She was hoping to shame him into letting her fly his Jenny.

He put his hands on his slim hips. "Can she?"

"Maximum speed 75 miles per hour. I don't think we were close to that." She had no way of knowing if they had been or not. "Rate of climb, 400 feet per minute; stall speed, 45 miles per hour; endurance, 2 hours 18 minutes; service ceiling, 11,000 feet." She scrunched her mouth sideways. "Am I forgetting anything? Wing span, 43 feet 7½ inches; height, 9 feet 10⅝ inches; fuel capacity 26 gallons." That should prove to him she knew enough to fly the Jenny even if she did learn it all from magazines and newspapers.

He stared openmouthed at her.

She tried not to smile at his surprise. "Tell me, do you prefer a tractor-style Jenny with the engine in the front or a pusher model with the engine behind you like the Maurice Farman?" When he still stared at her, stunned, saying nothing, she went on. "I don't think I'll ever fly a pusher. Too dangerous. Well, we have to be off. But we'll be back tomorrow. And, Lieutenant, tomorrow I'll be flying your Curtiss JN-4D."

She sashayed away. That would give him something to think about overnight. She climbed into the Ford and drove off without so much as a glance back at him.

❧

Pete stared openedmouth at Lizzie's retreating form. He'd watched her wave her arms and take in all there was to the flying experience. She'd even pulled the pins from the back of her hair and let it loose. She was the most surprising and complex doll he'd ever met. His gape turned to a smile. And he'd see her again tomorrow. He'd make sure he gave her more attention. But as far as her flying his aeroplane, that was out of the question.

❧

Lizzie drove as fast as she dared and stopped with a jerk in front of the post office. Daddy was standing on the sidewalk, glaring. Ivan scrambled over the seat into the back.

Daddy hobbled to the passenger door and opened it. He lifted his peg leg in and sat, then pulled his good leg in. "You better have a good explanation for being more than a half hour late."

"I'm so sorry, Daddy." She put the Ford into slow speed and jerked forward. Daddy glaring at her made her nervous. She usually drove very well. She was even considering teaching Ivan to drive. Daddy hadn't consented to that yet, but Ivan was working on him and would soon have permission.

"So, why were you late?" Daddy was not going to let it go

until he had a satisfactory answer.

And no answer she gave would be good enough.

"It was my fault." Ivan leaned forward and poked his head between them. "I talked Lizz—Elizabeth into taking me up the canyon to go fishing." He pulled the tip of his pole up to the front seat to prove his point. "It didn't quite work out. I didn't catch a thing."

She was thankful for Ivan's intervention. Daddy accepted his excuses more readily than hers. And it was true. Ivan had talked her into driving him up the canyon to fish, and she'd brought along a book to read.

Daddy crinkled up his nose and sniffed several times. "Smells like gasoline in here."

"Bill let me pump the gasoline. I guess I must have spilled some," Lizzie said, taking the blame for that one.

"That's why women shouldn't be allowed to do things like that. You just let Bill pump the gasoline from now on."

She nodded, hoping nothing further would be said about today. Bill often let her pump her own gasoline. And she and Ivan had taken turns today pumping gas, spilling on occasion. If Daddy only knew how much she knew about engines and machinery, he'd have a fit. Between Bill and her late granddad, they'd taught her plenty. More than a lot of men knew.

That night after Daddy had gone to bed, Lizzie pulled out her Bleriot monoplane design sheets and unfolded them carefully on her bed. She just had to finish her aeroplane now. After being in the air, she couldn't live the rest of her life trapped by gravity.

three

Lizzie rose the next morning and cooked a breakfast of eggs, bacon, and flapjacks. Then she dressed in her best Sunday dress and went out to the Ford. When she'd told Lieutenant Garfield she'd return today, she'd forgotten about having church. Ivan was already sulking in the backseat.

"Don't worry, Ivan. Daddy usually takes a good long nap Sunday afternoon. We can go over to the Johnsons' field then. But only for a short bit."

Ivan sat up straighter. "Do you think Pete will still give us free rides?"

"He might," she whispered as Daddy came out of the house and struggled into the front seat.

Ivan was turning out to be Lizzie's pal while still remaining on Daddy's good side. Now that Lizzie was an adult of twenty, Daddy was holding more tightly to her than ever. He regularly lamented that he would shrivel up and die the day she married and left him. There would be no one to care for him.

She knew he wasn't that bad off and her leaving wouldn't likely be his demise, but the guilt he heaped on was still effective. If she ever did choose to marry, her husband would have to be willing to live with Daddy. But more likely, she would become an old maid caring for Daddy.

At church, Lizzie struggled to keep her mind on what Pastor Littleman was saying. Would Lieutenant Garfield still be at the field? Did he have enough people to keep him busy all morning? Or had he tired of waiting for them and left? *Please, Lord, I know my request is selfish, but it's not only for me but for Ivan, as well. Let the lieutenant still be giving rides.*

23

She forced the ninety horsepower bi-plane from her thoughts and focused hard on the pastor's words. He was talking about freedom. Something she longed for.

After church Lizzie made lunch, then busied herself with the dishes until Daddy announced that he was going to go lie down. She finished in the kitchen as quickly as possible, then went looking for Ivan. She couldn't find him anywhere. When she went into her room, she found a pair of Ivan's trousers on her bed. She'd asked him for them. She didn't want to worry about a dress being indecent. She knew Daddy thought a woman wearing trousers was indecent, but she didn't care. She needed them today, and Ivan had been more than happy to let her borrow a pair of his. He'd done it before.

If he'd left these here for her, he'd left without her. That sneak.

She quickly changed and went outside. She was afraid if she started the Tin Lizzie, she'd wake Daddy. She could either walk or push the stupid thing away from the small farmhouse and start it down the road. She'd never tried pushing it without Ivan's help. The lieutenant likely already had someone to fetch his gasoline, so she walked. She could pick wildflowers on her way home. But she'd better get home before Daddy woke and caught her in trousers.

She ran most of the way there but stopped by a maple tree showing the first hints of fall color at the edge of the field to catch her breath. She saw two automobiles but no bi-plane. Suddenly from over the trees in the orchard at the far end of the field flew the yellow Jenny. By the time the aeroplane landed, she'd joined her brother in the small group. "You left without me."

Ivan shrugged, holding Fred. "I figured I'd come ahead to make sure Pete didn't leave before you could get here."

She put her hands on her hips. "Don't give me that. You came for yourself."

"I left you the trousers."

She gave him a soft punch in the shoulder. "Thanks."

The lieutenant jumped down, helped his passenger safely down, who looked like he was very glad to be back on the ground, then walked over to her. "It's a pleasure, Lizzie. Ivan told me you were on your way." He took her hand and kissed the back of it.

She took a deep breath, almost forgetting why she'd come. "Ivan was wondering if he could get another ride today, Lieutenant Garfield." So that wasn't exactly why she'd come, but if Ivan got a ride, she'd likely get one, too.

"Please call me Pete."

"That's rather bold."

He took a step closer. "Everything I do is bold. Call me Pete, and I'll take the boy up. And if you smile pretty for me, I just might take you up."

"Can I pilot it this time. . .Pete?" She gave him a big smile.

He smiled back, leaned toward her ear, and whispered, "No one flies my Jenny but me."

His warm breath tickled her ear.

"I have one more passenger to take up. Then it's Ivan's turn, and then"—he looked deep into her eyes—"it's your turn."

If she was a swooning type gal, that look might just do it. But she was immune.

Almost.

❧

Pete couldn't believe Lizzie's audacity. Did she really expect him to let her fly his baby?

He climbed up onto the wing ahead of her and gave her a hand up. He blocked the pilot's seat. "You sit in the front."

She poked out a pouty bottom lip.

A small part of him wanted to let her fly. A very small part. But he feared it was growing. No one flew his Jenny but him. He repeated the thought firmly to bolster his resolve. "No,"

"Can we do a loop?"

"I don't think so." That could make even experienced pilots squeamish.

"A roll then?"

"I don't think you're ready for that."

"What can you do to make the flight more exciting?"

"Get in, and I'll see what I can do."

She hesitated but climbed into her seat. . .up front. He checked to make sure she was properly strapped in this time. If he was going to do any kind of stunt, even an innocuous one, he wanted to make sure he didn't lose his passenger. "If I do a roll, will you give me a kiss when we land?" He couldn't believe he was even considering doing something that might be a little dangerous with her onboard.

"If you let me fly your aeroplane, I'll give you a kiss."

He straightened up and hit his head on the upper wing. "No." He climbed into his seat before she could argue further with him. He took off and did the same steep climb and dive he'd done with her yesterday, but this time he came much closer to the ground. Maybe that would scare her. He did more maneuvers with her than he ever did with any passenger.

He touched her shoulder, and when she turned, he shouted, "Are you doing all right?"

She grinned and nodded vigorously.

Against his better judgment, he did a single roll before bringing the aeroplane back down to the ground. A small compromise. Now maybe she'd quit asking to sit in the pilot's seat.

When Lizzie got out, she danced around. "That was so exhilarating. I want to go up again." She stopped in front of him and grabbed his upper arms. "You have to teach me to fly." Then she began dancing and spinning again.

So much for scaring her out of flying. He'd given a few people rides who'd gotten the bug and wanted to fly for themselves, but no one had been as excited as Lizzie. And she was a doll. He could understand gents getting the fever to fly, but a pretty little thing like Lizzie? His heart opened up to the dancing imp. With some instruction, he bet he could teach her how to fly his aeroplane.

What was he thinking?!

Not only was he not going to let her or anyone else fly his baby, but he wasn't going to be around long enough. Since he had left the service, he'd never stayed in any one place longer than five days. Except Spokane, and look at what trouble that got him into. Agatha. He hoped she'd figured out what to do.

"You didn't bring your Tin Lizzie. . .Lizzie."

She stopped twirling, but her smile never faded.

He stared at her a moment, then said, "I was hoping to get a lift into town to fill my spare tank." Kiss or no kiss, the sooner he left, the safer he'd be.

"I couldn't bring it. But I can tomorrow."

That was a relief. He could stay one more day and see Lizzie again. He shouldn't be, but he was glad he was going to.

"We have to go, Ivan."

Ivan sat on the ground playing tug-of-war with Fred and an old rag. "Only one of us needs to be there. Tell Dad I'm with my friends."

She planted her fists on her hips. "Ivan, that's not fair."

"I saved your skin yesterday."

Lizzie huffed and stomped her foot.

Ivan smiled. "See ya."

She turned and marched away.

Pete watched her storm off. He wanted to chase after her and make her smile again, but he just stood there. It was safer that way. "What was that all about?"

Ivan yanked on the rag and pulled it free from Fred's mouth, who immediately grabbed it again. "Nothing."

There was something. He could tell. He'd guess that their

father wouldn't approve of them flying in an aeroplane. Some people just couldn't keep up with modern inventions and appreciate them. "That was kind of mean of you to send your sister away and not go with her."

"She gets to come back all day tomorrow while I'm stuck in school. Then I got to show up at Liberty Orchard for work. We aren't quite ready for picking yet."

So he'd get to see just Lizzie tomorrow. "Picking what?"

"Fall is the apples. First the Reds then the Johnnys and Winesaps."

All types of apples, he supposed.

"Lizzie will be packing soon and working at the Liberty Orchard kitchen."

"Packing? Is she going somewhere?"

Ivan shook his head. "She packs apples at the warehouse; then she works making Aplets."

"What are Aplets?"

Ivan frowned at him like he should know, but he explained, "It's a chewy candy and oh so good. Lizzie gets to bring home some of the small end pieces that they can't sell."

"Sounds like I'm going to have to try some. Where are they sold?"

"Oh, you can't get any until they start making more in a couple of weeks. First we have to start picking, then the packing."

Pete could come back in a few weeks. But then it wasn't that long. Maybe he'd just stick around.

four

Sometime between Sunday night and dawn Monday, Pete woke to the sound of smacking. "Fred, knock it off." The noise continued. Why did the dog have to pick the middle of the night? "Fred!" he said more sharply.

Fred moved from his side on the blanket he'd stretched out on the ground under his aeroplane and started barking.

He groaned. "Fred, be quiet." He rolled over to look at him and stared at four hoofed feet inches from his face in the moonlight. He quickly backed away across the ground and stood up on the other side of Jenny. He took a deep breath and blinked a few times to clear his muddy mind and slow his heart rate from the sudden jolt. It was just a doe. He could easily run her off.

He took his cooking pot and a long-handled wooden spoon and rushed around the tail of the aeroplane, banging the spoon on the pot, yelling, and waving his arms in the air.

The doe startled and ran across the field. Fred gave chase.

"Fred, get back here." The dog obeyed immediately. "You're supposed to warn me before half my aeroplane is licked clean."

Fred wagged his stubby tail vigorously, looking up at his master.

"Come on. We'll fix it in the morning."

Pete didn't know how long he'd been asleep when Fred started barking again. The doe was back. Pete easily chased her off again and again.

The fourth time she returned and woke him, she'd brought another doe and a fawn with her. He'd had enough. He would chase her clear across the field this time so she knew not to come back. Just the movement of him throwing off his blanket and standing with a growl sent the three fleeing. He brushed his hands together. "And stay away this time!"

Fred began barking behind him, so Pete turned. A six-point buck looked considerably peeved with him. The buck snorted and pawed the ground.

Pete quickly scrambled under the tail and around and under the wing. The buck hit the tail with his antlers.

He cringed at the damage he knew the tail must have incurred.

Fred barked violently at the buck's feet.

"Fred, come here." The stupid dog was going to get himself trampled.

Fred backed away as the buck lowered his head toward him. Fred ran off across the field. The buck followed for a few yards, then stopped and came back.

Pete picked up his pot and spoon and caused a ruckus. It only angered the buck, who began ripping the fabric of the wing with his antlers while swinging his head back and forth. Pete tossed the pot and spoon down. Fred came back, and the buck charged at both of them.

Pete scooped up Fred, ducked under the nose of Jenny, and hopped up onto the wing, throwing Fred into the cockpit before he dove in. He straightened himself and saw the buck circling the aeroplane and snorting.

He patted the top of Jenny. "Hold on, Jenny. Hopefully, he'll leave soon."

But he didn't. The others returned.

Pete tipped his head back. *Lord, please don't let them ruin Jenny.*

❧

"I love you, Elizabeth." Daddy sat next to Lizzie in the Model T.

"I know, Daddy. I love you, too."

Daddy took her hand and patted it. "I don't know what I'd do without you."

She hated it when he said that. What he really meant was *Don't ever leave me.* She wanted to run as far away from him as she could. But at the same time, she wanted to hug him and tell him she would never leave. Mom had had enough of his suffocating love seven years ago and run off with another man, but she was killed in an automobile accident a few months later. Daddy didn't know Lizzie knew the truth. Daddy had told her and Ivan that Mom was visiting a sick aunt back East and had died there.

Mom's betrayal had injured him in a way he'd never recovered from. Lizzie did not want to be like her mom, so she knew she could never leave Daddy. So her life would have one of two outcomes: She would find someone who would marry her and could put up with living with Daddy, or she would become a spinster. She would likely be the latter. She watched him hobble inside the post office.

She wanted to hate him for manipulating her into staying with him the rest of his life and driving off any interesting young men who showed her attention. But she couldn't help seeing the lonely, bitter man he was becoming. A man who was afraid to be alone. He needed her. She felt trapped.

She finally drove away and headed straight for the Johnsons' field, afraid that Pete had gotten his own gasoline and flown away in the wee dawn hours before she could get there. *Please let him still be there.*

She pulled into the clearing and saw the yellow Jenny at the other end of the field. He hadn't left, but she didn't see him anywhere. A wadded blanket and tin cooking dishes were scattered around under the aeroplane. She turned off the Model T and pulled the hand brake back before getting out. When she slammed the door, Fred started barking from the cockpit. She looked up and saw Pete stirring with the ruckus Fred was causing. He appeared to have been sleeping.

She shaded her eyes. "You couldn't have been comfortable up there."

He stretched. "This wasn't by choice." He climbed out onto the wing and looked around the field. "I guess they're gone."

"Who?"

He jumped down. "Troublemakers." He rounded the other side of his craft and groaned. "It's worse than I feared."

She followed him. A hole ripped near the tail gaped open.

Pete pulled his hand out of the hole. "Frame's busted." He went over to the wing and slid his hand inside and along a three-foot tear. Under the wing, he found more tears.

"What happened?"

"Deer."

"What?"

"They like the dope the shell is coated with. This doe came up and started licking the wing. I woke up and shooed her away. She came back three more times. The last time with friends, another doe and a fawn. Fred and I ran them off, but when I turned around, I faced a particularly cranky buck that was determined to get a taste of my aeroplane. He wouldn't be spooked." Pete raked a hand through his messy brown waves. "I managed to grab Fred and climb inside. Last I saw when the sun was just coming over the rise, they'd finished with this wing and were starting on the nose." He rubbed his hand along the front of the aeroplane. "Licked clean."

"I didn't realize deer were such a danger. Good thing they don't fly."

He turned a withering look at her. "If I wasn't so tired and so mad, I might just laugh at that." He yawned. "I don't have enough dope to coat everything they ruined."

"I know where to get some." This was so perfect. Once she helped him repair his aeroplane, he'd be so grateful he'd have to let her fly the Jenny. "Give me your gasoline tank, and I'll fill it up while I'm getting the dope. Do you want to ride along?"

He sighed and shook his head. "I'd better stay and protect what is left of Jenny." He waved a hand toward the ground. "And clean up this mess."

Pete might be downtrodden now, but he would spring back when he saw all she was going to bring. Jenny would be good as new in no time.

❧

After Lizzie left, Pete folded his blanket and picked up his cooking gear. He stared at the badly dented pot. He hadn't realized he'd hit it so hard. At least his coffeepot was in good shape. He built a fire and started a pot of java, then took a closer look to inventory all the damage. He wouldn't be leaving any time today. . .or tomorrow.

Lizzie sure was cute, though. She was trying to be helpful, but he doubted she'd be able to find any dope in this two-bit town, if she even knew what it was. She might have some rote statistics memorized, but knowledge of the inner workings of a craft like this was a different thing, and understanding how to build one even rarer. He'd also need wood and nails to do some frame repair work. When she returned empty-handed, he'd see if he could talk her into taking him to Wenatchee. There was a slim chance he might be able to find what he needed there.

Soon Lizzie would return, and he would thank her for all her trouble and tell her how useful the stuff was that she'd brought—whatever it was. Then he'd tell her he needed additional supplies and ask if he could borrow her automobile to drive into Wenatchee.

He poured himself a cup of java and had swallowed the last of it when a Tin Lizzie motored onto the field. It stopped near him, and he waved to the four occupants. Two young men and two cute dolls piled out.

"See, I told you he was still here." The blond doll sidled up next to him and looped her arm around his. "Take me up first."

The brunette latched on to his other arm and leaned real close to his face. "Take me first."

The men glared at him.

He didn't care. He hadn't done anything to steal their dolls. "Sorry, ladies and gentlemen." He nodded to the men. "I can't take anyone up at the moment. Plane's busted up." He pointed to the damaged tail; then he forced a smile for each of the dolls. Since when did he have trouble flirting with ladies even on little sleep?

Just then, Lizzie drove up. He pulled free of the dolls and stepped away. "Sorry about the rides. Maybe in a few days."

He walked to the black Ford and opened the door for Lizzie as she turned off the engine. He hoped she hadn't seen that little scene with the dolls. He heard the other automobile drive away.

Lizzie climbed out and gifted him with a smile. "I'm back."

He thumbed back to the receding automobile. "Those were some people wanting rides."

"I could see."

So Lizzie had seen the flirting. "I wasn't interested in those dolls."

"Why not? Connie and Irene are both pretty."

"Because I'm not." Why was he defending himself? He shouldn't care who saw those dolls flirting with him, let alone Lizzie. But somehow it did matter. It was only because she'd offered to help him. That had to be it.

Mercifully, Lizzie changed the subject. "I brought a few other things I thought we might need to repair Jenny."

"We?"

"I'm going to help you."

"Oookay." He didn't know how much help she'd actually be, but he could teach her the name of a few tools, and she could hand them to him as he needed them. At least that way he'd get to spend a little more time with her, and maybe, just maybe, he'd get that kiss after all.

"First, I brought you breakfast. After the night you had, I thought you could use it." Lizzie took a metal top off of a metal plate.

Scrambled eggs, biscuits and gravy, and sausage. He took the plate. "Thank you." This smelled better than anything he cooked himself over the open fire.

"And this is coffee." She handed him something wrapped in a towel. "I could only get a milk bottle."

He unwrapped the small bottle. The java was still hot. "This is great." He could certainly use more coffee, and this probably tasted better than the mud he'd brewed.

He motioned toward his fire. "Would you like to sit?"

She smiled and sat on the folded blanket.

He sat on the ground. "Did you make this?"

She shook her head. "I picked it up at the diner in town after I got all the supplies."

"All the supplies?" He was interested to see what she thought he needed. He closed his eyes and offered up a short prayer of thanksgiving for the bounty he'd been given. He held up a forkful. "You want some?"

"I already ate." She petted Fred, who sat nearby, waiting patiently, brushing his tail on the dry fall ground.

Pete savored the first perfectly seasoned bite of gravy-covered biscuit. "Mmm." He took a bite of eggs and flipped some to Fred. Fred caught it in the air and gobbled it down. When he realized what he'd done, he looked up at Lizzie. "I hope you don't mind. We always share our meals."

"That's fine. I'll remember to bring extra so Fred can have enough."

Lizzie waited until he was through eating, then dragged him over to her automobile. "I brought the dope, a whole gallon, some wood to repair the tail—I think these should be the right size—nails, glue, tools, and everything else *we* should need."

Had he imagined it, or had she slightly emphasized we? Amazingly, she had brought everything he would need. "How did you know what to bring?"

She shrugged. "I just figured."

Was there another pilot in town whom she'd spoken to and who had everything Pete needed? "So where did you find all of this?"

"Around. Shall we get started?" She was purposefully being evasive.

Pete continued to be amazed all morning. He would ask for a tool, and Lizzie was right there to hand him the right one every time. He might be able to leave tomorrow after all. No. He should let the dope and glue dry at least overnight, maybe two. . .just to make sure.

At midafternoon, Ivan strolled across the field. "You're still here!"

"I had a little trouble with deer."

"Can I go for a ride?"

"Not today. Jenny still has some damage. It might be a couple of days before she's in good flying shape. I'll stick around and make sure you get another ride before I leave."

"Really?"

"Sure."

"Ivan, you've got to be hungry. I'll take you home." Lizzie left and surprisingly returned a half an hour later, alone, with food for Pete and Fred.

"Here. I brought these for you, too." She tossed him an armful of tarps.

He caught them, and a rush of breath pushed from his chest. "What are these for?"

"One's for the nose, one the tail, and the other two are for the wings." She pointed to each section of his aeroplane.

He raised an eyebrow in question.

She took a deep breath and held out her hands. "Don't you feel the change in the weather? The temperature is going to drop tonight. I didn't want Jenny to get cold."

He stared at her. Was she serious? He babied his craft, but to think it might get cold was taking it a bit far. "Lizzie, she doesn't get—" He cut himself off when she cracked a smile and struggled not to laugh.

"I was pulling your leg. I thought if you covered most of it, it would keep the deer away. I brought rope, too, to tie it down."

She was amazing. He'd never met a doll like her.

"I can't stay long, but if we hurry, I can help you get her covered."

He dropped the tarps to the ground. "I can manage later. Come over here." He stepped over to the wing.

"What?"

"Just come here. I want to show you something."

She cocked her head to the side. "Tell me what it is first."

"I have to show you." He patted the aeroplane near the wing. "Over here."

She finally came over and faced the connecting point between the fuselage and the wing. "What is it? I don't see anything."

He put one hand on the wing and the other on the body of the craft. "Turn around, and I'll show you."

She turned in place, and he leaned closer.

"What are you doing?" She put a hand on his chest.

"I think you know what I'm doing."

"Would you kiss a lady without her consent?"

"If I thought that was the only way to get a kiss from said lady." He leaned some more.

And before he knew it, Lizzie had dropped down and scuttled under the wing. He couldn't believe she'd done that.

"Patience," he heard her call from the other side of the wing.

He came around and saw her climbing into her automobile. He ran over and stepped up onto the running board as she pushed the starter and the engine growled to life. "Will patience get me what I want?"

She looked up at him and smiled. "It might."

"Then I shall be long-suffering."

She giggled.

"You don't believe me? I shall be so patient everyone will think a new unusual tree has sprung up in the field. That is how long I'll wait." He stepped off the running board and gave her a deep bow.

Her smile changed from a simple flirtatious one to something else. His heart skipped a beat, and something opened up inside him that he knew only she could fill. And he regretted pressing her for a kiss and chasing her away. He wanted her near him so he could drink in her zest for life. A zest he'd thought he'd had.

five

The next two days, Lizzie helped Pete with the repairs and then just stayed and talked with him while everything dried. He didn't seem to be in a hurry to get the work done.

Lizzie ran her hand along the repaired wing. "I think everything is dry."

Pete came over, reached an arm around beside her, and felt the dope on the canvas shell. "Feels dry."

She looked up at Pete, and he smiled down at her, his brown gaze wrapping her in a longing embrace. If he tried to kiss her right now, she'd let him.

"Lizzie, you really surprised me the last few days. You seemed to know everything to do to fix my aeroplane."

She drank in his compliment. She knew he threw compliments around to girls to charm them, but this was a real one. One he hadn't given lightly. "It wasn't really that hard." She wasn't ready to tell him her secrets. It was better to keep him guessing and wanting to know more.

"I know, but most dolls don't have the faintest interest in aeroplanes or how they work."

He was fishing for information, but his hook was going to come back empty. A small pang of jealousy surprised her at his mention of other girls he'd met. "They were only interested in the dashing pilot."

He gave her a cocky smile. "Who wouldn't be?"

"Me." She turned and walked away. She'd sized up Lieutenant Pete Garfield from the get-go. He used his charm, boyish good looks, and his tales of adventures to interest the ladies. She'd seen it while he offered rides to paying customers.

He was polite and cordial to the men, but he openly flirted with the ladies.

He grabbed her hand and pulled her to a stop. "Hey, don't try to fool me. You're interested in me. I can tell. I can always tell."

She wouldn't feed his ego by telling him he'd grown on her. "Maybe I'm only making you think I'm interested so you'll let me pilot your Curtiss."

He shook his head. "You can give up on that dream. Why don't you ask the other pilot to let you fly his aeroplane?"

"Other pilot?"

"The one you got all the supplies from."

He was fishing again. He didn't need to know just where she'd gotten everything. At least not yet. "Are you jealous?"

He released her hand, took a step back, and cleared his throat. "Of course not."

He was uncomfortable now. She liked throwing him off balance. "You said I surprised you. Do you like surprises?"

He took a step toward her. "Maybe."

She tipped her head back a little to look up at him. She sighed. He certainly was handsome. "I have something else that will surprise you."

"What?"

"Let me fly your Jenny, and I'll show you." She liked teasing him about flying his aeroplane. She didn't really expect him to let her fly it, but she did still hope.

He just stared at her.

Was he actually contemplating letting her in the pilot's seat?

He cleared his throat. "Shall we see if the tail's ready?"

She nodded, and he turned away. She took in an unsteady breath before joining him by the tail.

"She's ready to fly. You want to go up with me to test her out?" She was about to ask to fly it herself when he added, "In the front seat."

She folded her arms. "What if I say no unless you let me fly her?"

"Since you're not going to fly her, you can either ride up front or stay on the ground."

"Maybe I'm bored with just riding along."

He leaned toward her and whispered, "I promise to make sure the ride is anything but boring."

He'd done it. He'd pulled a smile from her when she was trying so hard not to look as eager as she was. "You drive a hard bargain." She climbed up into the front seat and secured the belt across her lap.

❧

Pete climbed up onto the wing at Lizzie's side, holding out the extra leather helmet and smiling triumphantly. She hadn't tried to sit in his seat. . .this time.

"Lieutenant Pete Garfield, don't think you've won. I fully intend to fly your aeroplane." She pulled the helmet onto her head.

He had no doubt about it. He just wasn't sure how much longer he could put her off. From the first time she sat in the pilot's seat, something deep inside him had known she'd fly this aeroplane. He just hoped he had the good sense to leave town before that "something" rose to the surface and got the better of him.

He leaned in and tugged on the edge of her belt. "I don't want to lose you up there." He climbed into his own seat and adjusted his belt.

Fred barked and rose up on his haunches.

"We'll be right back, boy. Go on. Wait by the Tin Lizzie."

Fred backed up when Pete started the engine.

He rolled the aeroplane forward, checking the wing and the tail, then he pushed the throttle hard and sped over the bumpy ground and was soon airborne. He circled the field, keeping an eye on the damaged wing. It seemed to be holding up, as was the tail. He banked right then left, climbed and dove. Jenny felt good. She was performing as well as ever.

He pushed the throttle hard right and flew with the wings up and down, a sort of sideways roll. He straightened out, then pushed Jenny into a steep climb, turned, and raced back to earth, leveling out before he got too close to the ground. Lizzie couldn't possibly be bored. But just to make sure, he performed a roll.

Clunk.

He felt it as well as heard it. He pulled out of the roll as the engine wound down and the propeller stopped. His gut twisted. This was not good. The camshaft had broken. It had happened to him before—a year ago—but that time he was flying alone, and the good Lord had provided a field Pete could quickly glide to and land on. Today he'd been showing off for Lizzie and had drifted too far away from the field.

The day he'd arrived with Finn, he'd circled the town to find the best place to land. Most of the area was covered with orchards. Precious few landing opportunities.

In his head, he calculated the distance from the field and his altitude, with the seven-to-one glide ratio of the Jenny. He thought he could just make it if those apple trees on the edge of the field were a hair shorter. But did he still have a seven-to-one ratio with the added weight of Lizzie? He had only one option. Try. *Lord, I could use a little help here.*

This is no time to panic. Take control of the craft and bring her down safely. He could do it. He had the skills. He'd never killed anyone and wasn't about to start today. Did Lizzie even realize they were in danger? *Lord, please don't let her be frightened.*

Her rote knowledge wouldn't give her insight into the purr and tempo of the engine. And hopefully she'd just think he was trying to impress her with a power-off landing.

Sweat from his brow dripped into his eyes and stung. He

wiped it away and focused on his target. *Keep her level and glide at as low a decline as long as possible.* The field was in sight, but he was too low. The last couple of rows of trees and his Jenny were about to become a pile of kindling.

He tried to pull the nose up to gain just a little lift.

No good.

They would hit the trees any second now.

He felt a branch tug at the left wheel. Suddenly, a burst of an updraft lifted Jenny over the trees and dropped her. She missed the trees but hit the ground hard. He hoped the wheels stayed attached.

Jenny rolled to a stop.

He took a deep breath and could feel his heart hammering the back side of his ribs as though it wanted to escape.

Lizzie climbed from her seat and onto the wing. "That was great! I wasn't a bit bored."

He wanted to say *I told you so*, but all he could manage was a stiff nod. She jumped down, and he climbed out and down and then kept walking. Away. He didn't want to look at Jenny. She'd almost killed Lizzie. He raked his hands through his hair and hunkered down somewhere in the middle of the field. But he shouldn't blame Jenny. It wasn't her fault. Actually, Jenny was the reason they were both alive. Her broad double wings had carried them down. It was that piece of junk OX5 engine poor Jenny was saddled with. It was no good. None of them were. He guessed he'd pushed the good Lord long enough with it. He needed to use some of his saved money and replace it. He'd meant to. But when it was just himself, he'd trusted in the abilities the Lord had gifted him with to compensate for the engine's weaknesses. He'd been frugal with his money and saved every bit of his stunt pay rather than gambling it away as fast as he earned it like so many freewheeling pilots did.

"Pete, what's wrong?"

He shot to his feet and turned. Lizzie's soft voice behind him startled him as much as if it were a gunshot. "Don't sneak up on me like that!"

"I'm sorry. I didn't mean to scare you."

He could still feel the adrenaline pumping through his veins. "You didn't scare me." He started walking toward Jenny. He wasn't quite sure why, but he stopped and turned back to Lizzie. "The camshaft broke."

She cocked her head to the side and pinched her eyebrows together.

"That could have been our last flight," he said.

"But you can fix it, right?"

He grabbed her by the shoulders. "We could have died. You could have died."

She smiled. "You're not much of a daredevil if one little mishap scares you so bad."

She was trying so hard to make him feel better he had to smile. It didn't bother him so much to risk his own life, but it was a whole different thing to risk hers. "Lizzie, I'm sorry I put your life in jeopardy."

She laughed. "You're not in control of the universe. God knew that was going to happen and got us down. I'm the one who wanted to fly. You didn't make me."

"You're not mad at me?" He was afraid he'd scared her off of flying forever.

"How could I ever be mad at you? If it weren't for you, I'd never have flown. Even if it wasn't in the pilot's seat." She turned her smile more coy. "If I help you get the parts you need to fix her, will you let me fly her?"

Yes, he would. He just wasn't going to let her know that yet. "No one flies my Jenny but me."

"We'll see." She turned and sashayed off.

Ivan waltzed up. "I'm ready for my ride."

Pete didn't take his eyes from Lizzie's retreating form. "Sorry, not today, buddy. I broke a camshaft. She won't be going up for quite some time."

Ivan moaned and kicked the ground. "I get all the bad luck."

"Say, Ivan, does Lizzie have a beau?"

"No," the boy said, downtrodden.

"No one she's promised to?" He tore his gaze from Lizzie climbing into the Tin Lizzie. "Your dad hasn't made arrangements for her to marry, has he?"

Ivan squinted up at him like Pete was a touch crazy.

That was a relief. Pete shook his head. What was he thinking, looking at Lizzie like he'd like to stick around forever? As soon as he fixed Jenny, he'd steal a kiss and fly away as fast as he could.

six

Lizzie lay in bed the next morning, unable to sleep any longer, thinking about what Pete had said. They both could have died yesterday. That was a scary thought, but the Lord had seen to it that Pete's skills and experience got them down safely. She'd thought Pete was just showing off. At the time, she'd chalked it up to his boast to keep the ride from being boring.

Dawn was just beginning to gray the horizon. Today she would really surprise Pete, and he'd have to let her fly his aeroplane after all the help she was going to give him to fix it . . .again.

She got up and began her chores, starting with laundry. She wasn't going to be able to go see Pete for some time. If she started now instead of after she took Daddy to work, maybe she could have everything washed and hanging to dry by noon.

She was taking the first clothes from the washing machine and cranking them through the wringer when she heard Daddy get up. She left the clothes and went to the stove to start breakfast. She had another load washing in the electric wringer washer by the time she left to take Daddy to work.

&

By midmorning Pete was tired of waiting. He pulled himself up from under the wing and brushed the dirt from his trousers. Lizzie had always come long before now, except when she had church. That was the one thing gypsying across the countryside didn't afford him, time in church. But he had his Bible that he read regularly, and he prayed. Still, it would be nice to be inside the walls of a church and have people who cared about him all around. Maybe someday he'd settle down and have that.

Lizzie had said the flight was fun and it didn't seem to bother her, but her absence this morning told him that, after the danger she'd been in yesterday had sunk in, she was scared. He was so glad he'd not allowed her to fly. That could have been a real disaster. Not that either of them would have been around to know it.

He patted his leg for Fred to come and pointed his feet toward the two-bit town he'd landed near. He had no idea where Lizzie lived. Would he see her in town? If he did, he'd hide because he'd know for sure she was avoiding him and he didn't want to embarrass her.

Cashmere was a quaint little town of a few hundred people. He walked the main street past a warehouse, a general store, a restaurant, the post office, and a few other businesses.

He stopped at a five-and-dime store, arrested by a display in the window. APLETS: THE CONFECTION OF THE FAIRIES. Around the sign were boxes of the treats and cutout cardboard fairies. Ivan said that Lizzie helped make Aplets. Then he saw it, a photograph of the Aplet fairies: four dolls dressed up in gossamer gowns and wings. He leaned closer and banged his forehead on the glass. That one looked just like Lizzie. Lizzie in wings. A poor fairy who couldn't really fly.

He continued to the other end of town and roamed the residential streets. No Lizzie. He was more disappointed than he'd thought he'd be. Now he really wanted to find Lizzie and make sure she was all right. No other doll had caused these feelings in him. No other doll had been as interested in aviation. He had to be careful what he said around her because she was so knowledgeable. She almost knew his Jenny as well as he did.

Almost.

Her knowledge had to be all head knowledge she memorized somewhere. It wasn't practical or from experience. Until you lived it, it wasn't real. He enjoyed watching Lizzie experience the real thing for the first time.

"I guess we're on our own, Fred." Lizzie wouldn't be helping with repairs this time. He kicked the ground. He should have test-flown Jenny first by himself. He walked back through town and headed toward the highway and the bridge that crossed the small river. He leaned against the railing and watched the water rolling by. Automobiles passed behind him at regular intervals, but he didn't give them more than a cursory thought.

One stopped and blew its horn. "There you are."

He turned and smiled at Lizzie. She was like a fresh spring rain.

Lizzie opened her door. "Come on, Fred."

Fred hopped in immediately.

She closed her door. "You have to come with me now. I have your dog."

He swaggered over. "Are you kidnapping my dog?"

"You, too. Get in."

"What if I refuse?"

"You'll never see your dog again." She rolled the car forward.

He jumped onto the running board, stepped over the door into the back, then over the seat into the front.

Lizzie laughed and sped up.

He fell back into the seat. "It's good to see you. I thought you weren't coming."

"I said I'd come."

"After yesterday I thought you might have been frightened off." He straightened himself.

"I don't scare so easily. I'm what you might call a modern woman."

"You think so?"

She nodded and turned onto a lesser-used dirt road and swung back around into town. "I'll show you that surprise now."

"If you don't mind me asking, why'd you wait so long to come?"

"I forgot that it's laundry day. I had to get the washing done and the clothes hung up. I can't stay long. I have to start taking the clothes down and iron Daddy's work shirts."

He'd heard her mention her dad a couple of times now, and he got the impression the man might not be happy with his little girl coming to see him. "Say, when I get Jenny flying again, how about I take your dad for a ride?"

Lizzie jerked her head toward him. "No!" She just stared at him.

"Lizzie, look out." He grabbed the steering wheel and jerked it, but they still ran off the road.

She slammed her foot on the brake pedal.

He threw his hands out to the dashboard and caught himself as the Tin Lizzie came to a sudden stop and the engine chugged off. "You can never be that careless when you fly."

"You can't tell Daddy I rode in your aeroplane."

So her dad would disapprove of not only him but also of what his daughter had been doing. Pete wasn't sure why. She hadn't done anything wrong. Though he was a bit concerned about her driving. That was twice that he knew of she'd run off the road.

"Promise me you won't tell him."

"I've never met your dad."

"It's actually best if you don't. Daddy doesn't even like automobiles, but we got this on account of his wooden leg. He can't walk from the farm to the post office where he works. If he knew I was up in an aeroplane, he'd have a fit. But I don't think he knows people can take rides in aeroplanes. He hasn't mentioned you being in town." She opened the throttle and pressed the electric start, and the engine came back to life.

He put a hand on her arm. "Lizzie, it's all right. You want me to drive?"

She took a deep breath. "No, I'm fine." She drove back onto the road.

"So where are your wings?"

Lizzie jerked her head toward him. "My what?"

He grabbed the wheel. "Keep your eyes on the road!"

"Are you this nervous when you fly?"

"No. Only when you drive. Maybe you should let me take over."

"I'm fine. What did you mean by my wings?"

"I saw an advertisement for 'the confection of the fairies,' and there was your picture."

She sighed, evidently relieved. "Oh, that. I was dressed up and on the Liberty Orchard float, as well."

"Have you always had this dream to strap on wings and fly?"

She nodded. "I always loved to watch birds soaring in the sky, and when I was fourteen, I read a story about aviation."

"You know most pilots are men. I can't name a single female pilot."

"A girl in Kansas named Kitty flew a heavier-than-air craft. Harriet Quimby flew over the English Channel in 1912. What about Katherine Stinson, Ruth Law, and Matilde Moisant? And Bessie Coleman went over to Europe to get her pilot's license. She couldn't get it here simply because of the color of her skin. And me."

Lizzie knew more than he did. But it took more than head knowledge to be a good pilot. It took skill, experience, and a natural aptitude. Few had the God-given gift. He was grateful when Lizzie pulled up to a garage and parked beside the building.

Good, a mechanic who might be able to help him with his camshaft. This must be where she'd pumped all the gasoline for him.

An old man who looked like he could have fought in the War Between the States came out wiping his hands down a pair of greasy coveralls. Pete nodded. His kind of man.

"Hi, Lizzie."

"Hi, Bill. You remember Lieutenant Pete Garfield, the pilot."

Bill shoved his hand out. "Nice to meet you again."

Pete shook the old man's hand. He remembered now. He'd taken the man up three times.

"Can we go around back? I want to show Pete."

Bill shoved his thumb against his upper teeth and gave them a push, then wiggled his lips around. "That's better. Let's go."

Pete followed Lizzie and the old man around the building to another structure that wasn't quite a building or a barn. It had a roof and three sides, and inside something very large was draped in a canvas tarp. This must be the surprise. And from the size and shape, Pete had a pretty good guess what it was.

Bill grabbed a corner of the tarp and slowly pulled it off the spindly frame of a monoplane.

Pete leaned toward Lizzie. "He's your pilot friend?"

She shrugged. "Could be your friend, too."

Anyone who was handing Lizzie her dreams to fly was going to be no friend of Pete's. He wanted to be her only means to fly. He wanted her to look only to him for the fulfillment of her hope to fly. But the aeroplane wasn't nearly finished. Lizzie wouldn't be going up in that any time soon. Besides, the old man might never finish it. A lot of people started aeroplanes and never got them off the ground.

He patted Bill on the back. "So you're building a Bleriot?"

Bill gave a shy smile then pointed to Lizzie. "It's hers."

"You're building it for Lizzie?" He did seem like a sweet old man.

"Shoot, no. I couldn't build nothing like this. Lizzie's building it. I'm just giving her the space to do it."

Pete turned to Lizzie. She smiled triumphantly, and he could feel his jaw hanging slack.

❧

Lizzie's insides were all bubbly as Pete stared at her with his mouth hanging open. "Surprise."

Pete pulled up his jaw and looked like he was going to form a word. His lips moved, but nothing came out. Then he shook his head.

She wasn't sure what to think. Was he impressed or not? "I've been working on it all summer. I thought I'd have it done, but it looks like I won't get to fly her until next summer."

Pete pointed to her aeroplane and tried again to say something but was unsuccessful.

She put her hands on her hips. "Well, I'll be. Lieutenant Pete Garfield at a loss for words. Let me help you. 'Darb, Lizzie. I'm so proud of you. Aren't you just the cat's meow.'"

Pete waved a hand toward the craft and again failed to speak.

She knew how to get him to talk and made her voice deep, pretending to be him. " 'Well, Lizzie, since you have your own aeroplane, I'd love to let you fly mine.'"

"No."

That did it. "You can speak."

"You are the other pilot in town? This is how you know so much about different aeroplanes? You are building a Bleriot?"

"Why is it so shocking? I understand lots of people are building them."

"Well yes, but a doll?"

She planted her hands on her hips. "Is there something wrong with a doll building an aeroplane?"

"No. I just never once imagined you building an aeroplane."

"Well, snap out of it, or I won't help you fix your Jenny.

Then you'll be permanently grounded and asking to fly my aeroplane."

A slow smile spread across his face, and he stepped closer. "I think I'll get my aeroplane in the air before you get yours."

She slapped him on the arm. "That's the spirit. Now I think our best shot at a camshaft will be in Wenatchee. I can drive us there tomorrow."

"Maybe you should let me drive?"

He'd been scared by her driving. She let a slow smile pull at her mouth. "I'll let you drive my Tin Lizzie if you let me fly your Jenny."

He held his hands out to his sides. "My life is in your hands."

She was disappointed he hadn't even stopped to think about it. She'd wear him down.

Pete ran his hand along the glistening frame. "I can see that you have it all framed, and it appears you have a varnish finish on it already. Are you following design plans?"

"I have them at home."

"What kind of engine do you have?" Pete walked to the nose.

"A Continental."

"Good. The more common fan and Y-type Anzani aren't as good."

That's what she'd read. It was good to have that confirmed.

He walked along the other side and studied her wing construction. "What's your next step?"

"I have all the cotton to cover the frame, but I'm not sure how to make it fit tight."

"Just pull the fabric as tight as you can, and the dope will do the rest. As it dries, it will pull it tight as a drum. Do you want me to help you get started wrapping it?"

"Sure." Tears stung the back of her eyes. To have Pete help her meant so much to her. A real pilot. Someone who knew what he was doing. Someone who'd done more than read about aeroplanes. She quickly turned away and went to the crate with all the cotton fabric in it. He'd never respect her as a pilot if he saw her cry.

❧

Pete stared at Lizzie standing near his Jenny. He'd spent two hours helping her put fabric on her Bleriot frame. They'd only gotten the tail fitted, but she was so happy. She had a smudge of grease on her cheek. She was absolutely incredible. He still couldn't believe she was building her own aeroplane. He doubted she'd ever get it in the air, but just that she would go against convention and even try. She was something else.

Pete took Lizzie's hands and, stepping closer, pulled them behind her with his own hands. "I'm going to kiss you, Lizzie Carter."

She smiled sweetly up at him. "No you're not."

His mouth pulled up on one side. "It looks like I am." A small voice inside said, *Just do it. Quick.* But he didn't.

She shook her head gently.

"Why not?"

"Because I don't want you to."

He groaned. "You sure do know how to spoil a guy's intentions." He loosened his grip on her hands, but she didn't try to free herself.

She kept her head tilted back, looking up at him. And her eyes. . .oh, those beautiful blue eyes, the color of the evening sky, begging him to kiss her. Or were they daring him to go against her wishes?

"I have to go now," she said in a lilting whisper but still made no move to free herself.

He released one hand and held the other as he walked her over to her Tin Lizzie, and she climbed in. He gripped the bottom edge of the open window. "Lizzie, why won't you let me kiss you?" He'd never once had this much trouble garnering a simple kiss before. Dolls usually threw themselves at him, giggling. He could have all the kisses he wanted, but Lizzie was special. He knew a kiss from her would be worth the wait. And he was determined to wait. As long as it took. He no longer wanted a stolen kiss; he wanted one freely given by Lizzie. One she would gladly return.

She smiled, put on her driving goggles, and pushed the starter.

So she wasn't going to answer him. "Lizzie, you are not nearly as modern as you like to think."

She let the Ford roll a few feet, then stopped and turned in her seat. "If I let you kiss me, then you'll fly away." The Ford was rolling again before she turned back around.

Keep your eyes on the road, he wanted to call after her but just stared at her receding automobile. Was she right? Would he leave? It's what he'd always done in the past.

Kiss and run.

seven

The next day, Pete stood in front of a diner in Wenatchee and watched Lizzie drive away. She was going to see a friend of her dad's and said she couldn't take him with her, but she'd be back for him in a bit and they'd go to a mechanic who could help them. He didn't want to stay at the diner because Fred would have to stay outside alone, so he walked toward the river. He'd be back before Lizzie returned. When he got near the train station, he saw a familiar, hunch-shouldered figure. Was Finn leaving? He hustled across the street with Fred on his heels and caught up with Finn inside the train station. "Finn."

The old-timer turned. "What are you doing here?"

"I was wondering the same thing about you. I'm only here because I saw you coming in here. Are you leaving?"

The old man looked down guiltily. "Maybe."

"Did you take care of your family business in Cashmere?"

Finn frowned. "I never said I had no family business."

"You said you had business to take care of and ever since I was a little boy and you traveled from one side of Washington to the other with me, you talked about having family in Cashmere."

Finn pursed his lips. "That's none of your business."

Pete could tell that Finn was running. He was all too familiar with that. Sometimes it was best for everyone if you just left. Other times, you needed to face whatever it was. He suspected it was time for Finn to finally face this one. "You can't leave until you do what you came to do. If you don't, you'll regret it."

The old man's stooped shoulders drooped even more than usual. "I just don't know if I can do it. I've done some things I'm not too proud of."

Had the old man been running from his past his whole life? "We all have regrets. Make this one less."

"Fred!"

Pete ignored the exclamation near him until two men knelt down and petted his dog. "How did you know his name?"

The older of the two men stood. He looked to be around thirty, a well-dressed, handsome blond man. "I'm sorry for the intrusion. As children, we knew a dog that looked just like yours, and her name was Fred."

The younger man, in his early twenties, picked up Fred and continued to pet him.

That was too much of a coincidence. "I, too, knew a female dog named Fred. This is her grandson. I named him Fred after her."

Fred was lapping up the attention as well as licking the younger man's face.

Finn pointed a finger at the other man. "And the female Fred belonged to a man named Conner Jackson, I bet."

"Yes," both Pete and the man said. They looked at each other.

"You are that troublesome boy, Burl Martin."

The blond man straightened his shoulders. "Burl MacGregor now. My sister and Ian adopted me as their son."

Finn pointed a gnarly finger at the younger man holding Fred. "And you must be little Miles." The younger man nodded but looked a bit confused.

Burl smiled. "And you are that man who was friends with Grandpa. Finn, right?"

Finn nodded. "I was so sorry when Arthur passed away. I just couldn't stay in Seattle no more. Are you still causing your sister grief?"

Burl shook his head. "Pa sent me to medical school. I'm a doctor. Miles is getting his training now, and then we'll have two doctors in the family."

Finn smiled. "How are your parents? And a younger sister, if I recall."

"Seven," Burl and Miles said in unison. Then Miles continued. "They could have at least given us another brother."

The train whistle blew. "All aboard," the conductor called.

Miles thrust Fred into Pete's arms, and Burl said, "We have to go. It was real good seeing you, Finn."

"Tell your parents hello from me."

"We will. They'll be glad to know you're doing well." The two men climbed aboard and waved as the train began to pull away.

Finn slowly turned to Pete. "Family's important, isn't it?"

"Very." Pete didn't have much, but he treasured his aunt. He missed her.

"All right. I'll go back to Cashmere and settle things, but I'm not going up in that flying contraption of yours."

Pete didn't need to tell Finn his aeroplane was broken. He'd never get the old-timer up in it again. "It just so happens, I can offer you a ride in a Tin Lizzie."

"Humph. That's almost as bad." Finn certainly didn't like machinery.

He and Finn walked back to the diner. Lizzie waited, leaning against her Ford.

"Hello again." She smiled at Finn.

Lizzie took Pete to a mechanic and got everything he'd need to repair Jenny.

As they drove back into Cashmere, Lizzie asked Finn, "Who are you going to see? I bet I know just where they live and can drop you off on their doorstep."

Finn tipped his well-worn hat. "No offense, miss, but I'd rather walk. I know my way." When she stopped in the field near Pete's aeroplane, Finn walked off.

"Finn doesn't like automobiles or aeroplanes. But he doesn't mind trains for some reason."

Lizzie nodded in understanding. "Daddy's the same way. He only tolerates the Ford because it's too hard for him to walk."

Lizzie helped Pete all afternoon until it was time for her to pick up her dad. He watched her drive away, wishing she could stay and missing her before she was out of sight. Why did this doll cause him pause?

ॐ

Lizzie drove the familiar road toward the farm. Daddy sat in the passenger seat as usual. She hoped he assumed she'd started at the warehouse packing apples. Daddy just knew that when it came time for apples to be packed, she'd be at the warehouse and then in the Liberty Orchard kitchen. He never asked her, so she hadn't had to tell him the truth. . .or lie.

When she stopped the Model T in front of the house, Finn got up from where he sat on the steps. What was he doing here?

"We don't take in no beggars," Daddy called as he opened the door and swung his good leg out. "Be off with you."

"Daddy, he's not a beggar." Lizzie got out and came around to the front stoop. "Finn, what are you doing here?"

He squinted at her. "You live here?"

She nodded.

"You a Carter?"

She nodded again.

"You know this vagabond?" Daddy asked, hobbling up to the steps.

"He's just an old traveler looking for his family." She took Finn's hand. "Let's go inside, and I'll fix supper."

Finn smiled at her, then gave a concerned look to Daddy. Daddy nodded. "Sure. You're welcome to share our table."

Had Finn come looking for her for some reason? Did he need help after all finding whoever it was he was looking for? And how had he found her?

❧

Pete had just thrown out the sludge in the bottom of his coffeepot and was getting ready to turn in for the night when he heard an automobile across the field, heading toward him at a reckless speed. It had to be Lizzie. He ran over before she got out.

"Oh, Pete." She threw her arms around his neck. "It was awful."

He held her for a moment as she cried on his shoulder. He found he liked holding her, comforting her. "Lizzie, what is it?"

She pulled away and dried her cheeks with her palms. "It's Finn."

Concern knotted his gut. "Is he hurt?"

She shook her head. "I can't find him."

"Don't worry about him. He goes off all the time. He comes and goes as he pleases."

She shook her head harder. "You don't understand. He's my grandpa."

"What?"

"He came to the house and had supper with us. Then he asked Daddy to forgive him. Daddy threw him out and told him never to come back. It's *my* family he was looking for."

Finn was family to Pete. Not by blood, but he'd been around off and on since Pete was five. "Mind if I borrow your automobile?"

"I'm coming, too."

"Can I drive?" Her heightened emotions and her carelessness behind the wheel were not a good combination.

She nodded, then climbed in through the driver-side door and slid over. He got in and drove toward town. After an hour of driving around, including a trip up the road toward

Wenatchee, they still had found no sign of Finn.

"Where do you live?"

"Up that way."

Pete headed the Ford in the direction she'd pointed, not too awfully far from the field he occupied.

"I don't think he'd go back there. Daddy was very firm when he told him to leave."

"I'm taking you home. We aren't going to find him tonight."

"I don't want to go back. Daddy's being unfair." Her voice was laced with defiance and anger.

"You have to go back." Her dad was probably worried about her, and Finn had always taken care of himself just fine.

"That doesn't mean I have to like it."

He pulled up to the house and got out, handing her the keys. "I'll see you tomorrow, and we'll find him." As he started to walk away, the front door opened.

"Lizzie, is that you?" said a concerned male voice. Probably her dad.

Pete instinctively stepped back into the shadow of a nearby tree. Lizzie went inside without saying a word to her dad. He watched the light and shadows move inside.

So Finn was related to Lizzie. Pete somehow had always known that his bond with Finn had been orchestrated by God. Because of that, he felt a responsibility to look out for Finn.

≈

The next morning, Lizzie worked extra hard at avoiding Daddy. She made his breakfast but left the kitchen when he came in to eat. Then she sat in the Model T until he was ready for her to drive him to work.

"Elizabeth, I hate you being mad at me. I'm trying to protect you. He'll only hurt you. You don't know how heartless he is. He's a cruel man."

She couldn't look at him, and she ignored his pleas all the way into town. Daddy got out at the post office, and when he shut the car door, she said, "I'm going looking for him."

Daddy's voice got hard. "I'm ordering you not to. He's not worth it. It's better this way."

"He's family."

"He gave up that right when he got Mom pregnant, refused to marry her, and left town with Grandfather's money. That's not the kind of family we need."

Finn didn't seem like he was the kind of man to do any of those things. "I have to find him." She drove off before Daddy could protest any further.

Tears stung her eyes. She really needed to talk to Finn. She wasn't naive. She knew that looks could be deceiving, but she also realized that people could change. Maybe Grandpa had been everything Daddy said, but she didn't believe he was that way now.

Lizzie spent the whole morning looking for Finn with Pete to no avail. Pete had convinced her that Finn would be all right. That he'd turn up in a week or so.

She spent Friday helping Pete repair his aeroplane. The camshaft worked, and Pete took her flying after he'd taken a solo test flight. Then on Saturday she and Pete went to Bill's Garage to work on her aeroplane. Her excitement to see her aeroplane come along was dampened by Finn's disappearance.

Bill gave her a gummy smile. "It's about time you came 'round."

"If you've been expecting me, then where are your teeth?"

He ducked his head shyly, then said, "I have somethin' for you."

She followed Bill, and Pete followed her inside and upstairs to his living flat. He motioned toward his bed. Finn lay across it with a whiskey bottle on the floor near his hand. "He's been pretty canned up for two days."

Lizzie ran over to him and took his hand. "Is he all right?"

"Once he sleeps it off, he'll be fine if I can keep a bottle out of his hand."

Pete came over and put his fingers on Finn's throat. "There's nothing you can do until he wakes up. Let's get that fabric on your aeroplane."

They'd covered the nose and part of one wing by mid-afternoon when Bill strolled out with Finn. "He's had a good, strong cup of coffee and some food."

Lizzie ran over and hugged Finn. "I was so worried about you."

Finn gave her a little smile. "It's been a very long time since anyone's been worried about me."

"I don't understand why Daddy hates you so much. He said you wouldn't marry Grandma."

Finn frowned. "Lilly and I were married! Her father didn't approve and kept Lilly from me. He said he was going to dissolve the marriage. Lilly was pregnant. After she had the baby, we were going to run away." A tear slipped from Finn's eye. He turned to Bill. "Where's she buried? I couldn't find her."

Lizzie believed Finn. She had one dim memory of her great-grandfather. Scary man. "I'll take you."

The four climbed into the Model T and drove to the cemetery. Finn wept at the grave of Lillian Carter. Beloved daughter. No reference to being a wife or mother.

Great-grandfather hadn't given Daddy his father's name.

Next to Lilly's grave was a joint grave: Robert and Esther Carter.

Now she knew why Daddy was so bitter. Great-grandfather had raised him that way. Then her mother's actions had hardened that feeling in place.

੩

Pete was getting too wrapped up in Lizzie. He hadn't thought about leaving in three days. He had to fly into the horizon and not look back before roots took hold and tethered him to the ground. But there was one thing he had to do first, or he'd always look back.

He helped Lizzie get her helmet on, then assisted her up onto the wing. Lizzie climbed into the front seat without fussing about wanting to fly. He grabbed a wire and jumped up onto the wing. "I think you're in my seat."

She smiled up at him. "No, I'm—" She sucked in a breath. "You're going to let me fly her?"

"I think I'm crazy, but yes."

She scrambled out of the front and into the pilot seat. It suited her. She had more flying knowledge than some pilots he knew. Why hadn't he let her fly it before? He knew. Letting her fly was his farewell to her.

"Let me go over a few things."

"I know what I'm doing."

"What you think you know up here," he tapped her head, "is not all you need when you're in the air. You have to be smart and make decisions no one has told you about. Your real learning will come from Jenny herself. She's a good machine. Trust her."

"I will."

Pete had her explain what every instrument told her, what it meant, and what everything was for. "I think you're forgetting something."

She shook her head. "No, that's everything."

He reached in and pulled up the loose end of her belt.

"Oops. I'm just so excited to get to fly."

"Carelessness up there," he pointed toward the sky, "will get you killed." He'd seen her drive.

"I'll be careful. I promise."

"If you aren't, I'll climb back here and land her myself." He could do it, too. "And don't try any stunts."

"I promise. Don't look so glum. I'm not going to crash her."

"I know." He was glum because he wouldn't see Lizzie after today. He climbed in the front. He was going to miss Lizzie. He buckled his belt and pulled on his helmet. This was strange—being in front and not having the controls at hand.

Lizzie rolled Jenny forward and ran her down the field. He gripped the sides of the opening. He didn't like this loss of control one bit. He wanted to yell for her to stop, but it was too late. If they didn't take off now, they would never stop before hitting the trees. Now he knew what his passengers felt like. Out of control and petrified.

He braced himself and felt Jenny leave the ground behind. Usually that was a glorious feeling, but not being in control made it a mite uncomfortable.

Lizzie flew up over the trees. He drew in a relieved breath. She circled the field. Three times. Each circle larger than the last. He'd told her to circle only once, then land. But he couldn't blame her. Once you were airborne, you never wanted to come down.

He pointed out across the buildings of Cashmere. She nodded and flew over the town. He made a U with his finger, and she turned back. He expected her to land, but she circled the field three more times. He finally pointed toward the ground. She stuck out her bottom lip but complied when he pointed more firmly.

This would be the tricky part. Landing was harder than taking off or flying. But Jenny was built to handle in-experienced pilots. She was a training machine. And Lizzie was not the type of doll to panic. He hoped she remembered everything he'd told her about how to approach the field and land. He wished the engine and wind weren't so loud so he could remind her.

Lord, please have her remember everything and make a controlled landing.

She made a wobbly approach over the orchard but came

down over the trees at a good descent. Once beyond the apple trees, she dropped Jenny nearly to the ground, then pulled up. He held his breath. Down, and the wheels barely touched the ground. He exhaled, but then they were up again. Then the jerk of the wheels grabbing for the ground. Then back in the air.

Just keep it down. It didn't have brakes like an automobile. It had to stop on its own, whether by the pull of the ground or the push of the oncoming trees.

The wheels finally stayed on the ground, and Jenny rolled to a stop a bit closer to the trees than he was comfortable with but in no danger of hitting them.

He heard Lizzie climbing out as he took several deep breaths. Not too bad for a first flight. Any flight that ended with everyone and the aeroplane in one piece was not too bad. He climbed out and joined Lizzie on the ground.

Lizzie grinned from ear to ear. "I felt like I died and went to heaven."

He knew the feeling.

"Is that how it feels every time? It was so thrilling. I have to go tell Ivan that I flew your Jenny. He's going to be green with envy." She ran to her Ford and opened the door, then turned and ran back. "Thank you. Thank you so much." She ran off and jumped into her Tin Lizzie.

He caught up to her as she started her engine. "One more thing." He leaned inside the Ford, unhooked her helmet, and took it off. For half a second, he thought about stealing that kiss, but it wouldn't be fair when he was leaving without telling her.

"Oops. Sorry." She waved and drove away.

"Good-bye, Lizzie," he said when she was almost out of sight. He would miss her, but now he was free to leave.

He packed his few belongings, fueled Jenny with his spare tank, put Fred in his harness, and climbed in. It was best if he left now and found another field to sleep in rather than wait until dawn. He didn't want to risk Lizzie returning.

❧

Ivan was sitting on the porch when Lizzie drove up. "I flew, Ivan, I flew."

Ivan shrugged. "So did I."

"No, I mean I actually piloted the aeroplane."

"No way."

"Pete let me."

"You what?" Daddy's soft voice behind her made the hair on the back of her neck rise.

She spun around. There was no sense denying it. "I flew a JN-4D aeroplane."

"I heard that gypsy pilot was still hanging around town. And you've been going to see him?"

"Daddy, he's not a bad person."

"Just like you think my father isn't a bad person?" Tears pooled in Daddy's eyes. "That flyboy's going to steal you away from me, and I'll never see you again."

"Daddy, don't. I'm not going anywhere."

Daddy hung his head and trod up the five steps. He turned at the door. "Just promise me one thing: that you'll never, ever touch a flying contraption or ride in one again. I couldn't handle it if anything were to happen to you." Daddy looked so sad.

"Nothing bad is going to happen."

Daddy's eyes drooped. "We'll see." He turned and walked inside.

She looked to Ivan.

"I'd hate to be you."

"Why?"

"Come on. You know. Dad's playing you like he always does. He looks sad, so you feel guilty and do whatever he wants to make him happy again."

She did feel responsible for Daddy's happiness. She just wished there was a switch like for electric lights and she could turn Daddy's happiness on and keep it on. If she left Daddy, she wasn't sure he would really be all right.

She climbed the steps and went inside. Daddy sat at the table with his hands folded and his head resting on them. She couldn't tell if he was praying or just thinking. "I'll start supper."

Daddy raised his head slowly. "I'm not hungry."

"You need to eat."

"I'm just going to turn in." Daddy rose slowly and shuffled his good foot toward his bedroom.

She slumped into a straight-backed chair. Daddy sure knew how to dampen her spirits. Even if he was manipulating her to keep her close, what was she to do? She couldn't just abandon him. Like Mom. Who else would care for him and make sure he ate well? Wash and mend his clothes? He needed her.

She sighed.

eight

The next day, Lizzie dropped Daddy off at work without a word from him about the previous night. He said nothing at all. He just looked out the passenger window and ignored her.

"Daddy, I'm sorry." She wasn't sure why she said that for she hadn't done anything to be sorry for. Daddy was mad she'd ridden in an aeroplane, but she'd never be sorry for that ride. She was sorry that it hurt Daddy. "Daddy. Please don't be mad at me."

He let out a heavy breath. "I work my fingers to the bones. My leg hurts from this hunk of wood. My hip and back hurt, too, because of it. My shin hurts where it was crushed. I don't know how that's possible when it's been gone for years. And the thanks I get from you is betrayal."

"I'm not betraying you. He's a good, decent, honest man."

"He's not right for you, Elizabeth."

"How do you know? You haven't even met him."

"I know his kind. He's a gypsy. Gypsies always leave." Daddy climbed out and hobbled with more of a limp than usual.

Was he really hurting today? Or was the limp for her benefit? She could never tell. She really needed to see Pete, so she drove out to Johnson's field. The yellow bi-plane wasn't there. Her heart sank.

Every day for the past two weeks, it had been right there. She drove to the end of the field Pete usually camped at. Nothing. She set the brake and climbed out of the Tin Lizzie, then walked over to the ring of rocks he'd used for his fire pit. The rocks were kicked over and out of place. She bent down

69

and felt the ashes. Cold as the rocks around them. There hadn't been a fire here all night. She looked to the sky. A single tear slipped down her cheek.

Pete was gone.

She hated that Daddy was right. She went back to the Ford and climbed in. Why hadn't Pete told her he was leaving? Had he known he was leaving when he'd let her fly?

Just then, she heard the distant rumble of the familiar OX5 engine and Jenny came into view.

Lizzie's heart skipped a beat. Pete. He hadn't left after all.

Pete made a perfect landing and stopped right by her. Unlike Lizzie's bouncy landing. She would have to work on that. Maybe she could talk him into letting her fly his aeroplane again.

Pete jumped down with Fred, pulled off his helmet, and ruffled his brown, wavy hair. "You're a sight for sore eyes."

So was he. She wasn't even sore about Daddy being sour at her now that she'd seen Pete. "Can I fly her again?"

Pete hesitated, and she could tell he was about to turn her down.

"Please."

"Jenny's running a little rough. Can you wait a day or two until I figure it out?"

She was disappointed, but he hadn't said no, and that meant he'd be around for a few more days. "Can you at least take me up?" She needed to be in the sky.

Pete hesitated again, then nodded. "No stunts, though. Just an easy ride. And we stick close to the field."

She climbed up onto the wing and stared at the full front seat.

Pete was right behind her. "Let me get my equipment out of there." He pulled out a backpack and a duffel bag and tossed them to the ground, then handed her the spare helmet.

She climbed in, and soon they were airborne. Just as Pete

said, it was a gentle ride around the field. She could hear what Pete meant about the engine running a little rough if she listened for it. She leaned back in her seat and closed her eyes. All of her worries and heartaches seemed to melt away up here.

When they landed and Pete helped her down off the wing, she said, "It sounds like a spark plug to me."

Pete smiled. "I thought so, too." But Pete wouldn't let her help him remove the faulty plug, not because he didn't think her capable, but because he didn't want her to get grease on her dress.

Pete drove her Model T to Bill's, then helped her tune the Continental engine on her aeroplane. "Hand me a wrench."

She held onto the tool. *He's a gypsy. Gypsies always leave.*

He turned to her. "That's the right one."

She handed it to him. "Pete, how much longer are you going to stay in Cashmere?"

"I have no idea." He shrugged and went back to work.

No idea? Couldn't he have said he loved it here or he never wanted to leave?

Pete took considerable time making sure her engine was running at its very best. When he was done, he stepped back and took a long look at her aeroplane. "I still can't believe you built that Bleriot all by yourself."

"I only had to follow the instructions. How hard is that?" Bill had helped her find an inexpensive used engine and all the scrap lumber she needed. She'd used every penny she'd earned and saved over the past three years to build it.

"I think there are people who would have a hard time following their nose if it weren't attached to their face."

There were people who didn't seem to have lick of common sense.

"Lizzie, I love you."

She smiled. He certainly did know what to say to try to

charm a girl. "I don't believe you."

He slapped his hand onto his chest. "You wound me. Why would I lie?"

Oh so charming, but she wouldn't be suckered. "To get what you want."

He cocked his hip against the side of her aeroplane. "And what is it you think I want?"

"A stolen kiss."

He was silent. "I would never lie to you, Lizzie. Never to you."

"All of your stories about fighting the Germans? All the aeroplanes you shot down? Being an ace pilot? Is all of that true?" She only wanted the truth.

He gazed at her a long moment. "I trained at Kelly Field at San Antonio in Texas. I was shipped across the Atlantic Ocean in October. I went through advanced training at a field in England. I was due to ship out to the Western Front on November 12, 1918."

"But the armistice was signed on the eleventh."

"The Great War was over. I never even got to ship over to Europe. I wanted to fight for my country. . .for the world. . . for freedom."

" 'Greater love hath no man than this, that a man lay down his life for his friends.' "

"Is that your measure of love? Death?"

"It's God's. If my life were in peril, would you put yourself in harm's way to protect me?"

He paused and thought. She appreciated that. He wasn't going to give her a flippant answer he thought she wanted to hear. He was searching for the truth, not only for her, but for himself as well. "I know the right answer, and I want to say yes. I'm just not sure."

"That's an honest answer. I like that."

"I think I would, but I would never really know for sure unless you were in danger."

"You were willing to die for strangers half a world away."

"It didn't really matter. I was doing it for the glory." He put his hands on her upper arms. "Now I have someone I want to live for."

"Another honest answer. You're full of truthfulness today."

He smiled. "I guess I am. So you can believe me when I say I love you." He stepped closer.

She had seen a change in him today with the truth. It was in his warm brown eyes. She believed him this time when he said it. She'd seen the real Pete Garfield. "You aren't going to kiss a lady without her consent, are you?"

He leaned closer and whispered, "If it's the only way I can garner a kiss from said lady."

"What happened to long-suffering?"

"Haven't I suffered enough?"

"You haven't suffered at all." She walked out to her Ford and sat in the driver's seat.

Pete stood next to her door. "Mind if I drive?"

She gazed up at him with the blue sky framing him. "You don't trust my driving?"

"You drive fine when you're watching the road. I just don't get to drive much. It's a nice change."

She scooted over. It was also a nice change from always being the one driving.

Pete got right to work at replacing the spark plug in the Jenny with the new one they'd gotten from Bill. And he still wouldn't let Lizzie help, so she leaned against the tail of Pete's plane.

He's a gypsy. Gypsies always leave. Pete was different. Wasn't he?

Pete put his tools away. "Let me take her for a test flight. Then I'll take you up."

It was time to let him go. "You may kiss me now."

Pete put a palm flat on either side of her on the aeroplane. "Are you trying to get rid of me?"

Maybe. Sort of. "No."

"You said if you let me kiss you that then I would fly away. Why the change of heart?"

"I want you to stay, but if you are only staying to get a kiss, I want you to leave now before my heart is broken like my grandma's." Pete had said he loved her, but how many girls had he said that to? A lot? Was she the only one? His bout of honesty had wrapped around her heart and taken her airborne. But for all that, he was still a gypsy flyboy who needed to be in the air and move from place to place.

He stared at her. Was he going to kiss her or not? She suspected he was going to play games with her. She needed him to get it over with and fly away for good if that was what he was going to do eventually. She rose up on her tiptoes and pressed her lips to his. Her heart hammered hard against her ribs.

He leaned in and kissed her back, pressing her against the Jenny. After a long moment, he pulled away. "You cheated."

"You never told me not to kiss you." She tried to duck under one of his arms, but he pulled her close.

"Not so fast." He kissed her again. "I'll be here tomorrow when you come looking for me."

Would he? Or was he once again telling her what she wanted to hear?

The following morning, Lizzie came and was glad to see Pete's plane still in the field. He hadn't left. Was he staying for her? Had he really meant it when he said he loved her?

"Your good sheriff paid me a visit last night."

That was strange. "Really? Why?"

"He told me I'd overstayed my welcome."

"He asked you to leave?"

Pete nodded.

Her stomach knotted. "Are you going to?"

"I've done nothing wrong. Mr. Johnson doesn't mind my using his field. I don't see why I should have to go."

She gave a mental sigh of relief at that.

❧

Two days later, Pete drove Lizzie's Tin Lizzie from Bill's Garage back to his aeroplane. It was time for Lizzie to go pick up her dad from work and go home. He didn't want to part from her. He'd tried to leave several days ago, but when he'd taken off from a neighboring field the following morning, he'd told himself he was only going to fly over once. If Lizzie was in the field, he'd land. He'd flown over the empty field then away. When he'd gotten to the point where he had just enough gasoline to make it back, he decided to fly over one more time. The first time hadn't been fair. Lizzie was never there that early. When he'd seen her in the field, Jenny seemed to land herself.

Every day, he told himself that this was his last day. He would leave. But every morning, he anxiously waited for Lizzie's return, and his heart sped up to a smooth cruising altitude when she finally showed up.

Three automobiles followed them across the field and stopped next to Jenny. "Looks like I have some new business. I still have enough daylight for a few runs."

As he pulled to a stop, he waved, but the seven men scowled as they stepped out of the automobiles. The sheriff stepped forward.

This was not going to be good.

"Lieutenant Pete Garfield?"

The sheriff already knew that, so why did he frame it like a question? Pete nodded.

"Is this your aircraft?"

Again, the sheriff knew. "Yes."

Lizzie stepped forward. "Sheriff Sherman, what's this all about?"

Pete figured it was harassment because he hadn't left town as ordered.

The sheriff waved her back. "Never you mind about this.

You run on home, Elizabeth." Sheriff Sherman turned back to him. "You mind if we search it?"

Pete rolled his eyes and waved his arm toward Jenny. "Be my guest." They would anyway if they had a mind to.

The sheriff nodded toward another man who climbed up on the wing as the other men moved around behind Pete. What was going on? He had a really bad feeling about this. What was the sheriff up to?

The man didn't search at all but simply reached into the front seat and pulled out a whiskey jug. He jumped down and handed it to the sheriff.

Sheriff Sherman uncorked it and gave it a sniff. "Bootleg whiskey. You realize it's illegal to transport or sell alcohol?"

Pete was surprised that the sheriff didn't at least try to look a little surprised since he or one of these other good men likely put it there. "It's not mine. I don't know how it got there." Not that he really expected them to believe him.

"That's true," Lizzie chimed in. "I was here earlier with him, and it wasn't in the aeroplane then. We have been in town together all day. He couldn't have put it there."

One of the men grabbed Pete's wrists and pulled his hands behind his back. He didn't bother to fight back. It wouldn't do any good. His wrists were quickly shackled together.

Lizzie turned on the man holding him. "Let him go. You can't do this."

Pete caught her gaze. "Lizzie, it's going to be okay. Don't worry about me. Remember that I love you."

Tears pooled in Lizzie's beautiful blue eyes. "I love you, too."

Pete's heart blossomed with those words.

"Sheriff Sherman, I have never once seen him with any kind of strong drink," Lizzie pleaded.

"Elizabeth, go home." The sheriff nodded to another man who grabbed Lizzie by the arms and pulled her toward her Ford.

She struggled. "Let me go!"

Pete tugged against his restraints. "Leave her alone."

Lizzie fought harder, and the man wrapped his arms around her from behind and lifted her, carrying her to her automobile. Lizzie yelled and made a ruckus.

"Ow! She bit me!"

He fought harder. "Don't hurt her. Leave her alone." He freed himself from the man who was holding him. He had to help her. Two men tackled him and pinned him to the ground. The air was forced out of his lungs when he hit the ground.

Lizzie's scream for him was quickly muffled.

Another man climbed into the driver's seat of Lizzie's Ford and drove off with her held in the passenger seat.

Pete tried to free himself.

The sheriff leaned down. "Don't make this worse on yourself."

Pete settled down. Lizzie would come see him. He believed that with all his heart. She loved him. And that feeling was better than any aerial stunt he'd ever completed.

&

Lizzie struggled against the fleshy bands around her that held like steel.

Deputy Otis Green, driving her Ford, pulled up to her house and stopped with a jerk.

As soon as they left, she'd leave, too.

Otis got out and opened Deputy Anthony Elmer's door. Anthony said to Otis, "Go get us another vehicle. I'll make sure she stays put."

"You can go with him and leave me alone." She wanted this brute to let her go.

"And bring her daddy back with you." Anthony carried her inside and set her in her mom's rocking chair. "We can do this the easy way or the hard way. You can sit nicely, like a lady, in that chair, or I can tie you to it."

She believed he would do it, so she folded her arms and glared at him as he sat in Daddy's chair across from her.

Pete had nothing to do with that bootleg whiskey. Someone else had put it there. If the sheriff would only let her talk, she knew she could make him believe her.

She heard what she thought were two automobiles driving up. Daddy came in, and the deputy left. She ran to Daddy and hugged him.

He put his arms around her. "It's going to be all right."

"Daddy, I'm going to the jail and see him."

"I'll come with you."

"Thank you." She hugged him again.

Ivan was walking up the road as they were driving into town. She stopped. "Pete's been arrested. You want to come?"

Ivan climbed over the door and fell into the back.

When she arrived at the jail, she ran in, leaving Daddy and Ivan to trail behind her. "Sheriff Sherman, I want to see Pete."

"I'm sorry. The prisoner can't have any visitors right now."

Daddy spoke up from behind her, "Lou, we've known each other for a long time."

"Thirty-two years."

"Can't you bend the rules this once and let Elizabeth see the boy?"

"I'm sorry, Tom. What kind of law enforcer would I be if I showed favoritism? I'm going to have to stand my ground on this." He didn't look sorry at all. Smug was more like it.

"But he didn't do anything wrong," Lizzie said. "I'll testify to that. I was with him all day. I just want to see him for a minute."

The sheriff shook his head.

Lizzie looked at Daddy, who'd given up on Pete so easily, but then, Daddy didn't care about Pete as she did.

She wanted to scream and yell and fight her way in to see Pete. She might be able to get around one deputy, but not two and the sheriff. Daddy wouldn't fight for her, and Ivan would be too scared. She turned in disgust at them all and stalked out. She'd be back tomorrow, ready for battle.

nine

Pete sat on the uncomfortable cot with Fred curled next to him. The mattress did little to disguise the wire and springs below. Where was Lizzie? Why hadn't she come?

He stood and paced to the bars, gripping them in his hands and looking out. A door sealed the end of the corridor. He was cut off from anyone coming into the main office.

Fred gave him a small whine of protest from the other side of the bars.

Pete scowled. "Get back in here."

Fred squeezed back through the bars and sat, looking up at him with his stubby tail brushing the dirty cement floor.

"Do you need to go out, boy?"

Fred went back down on all fours and wiggled back through the bars, turning to see if Pete was following, then sitting down to wait for him.

"All right. I'll see what I can do." Pete looked toward the door. "Hello? Can anyone hear me?" He called several more times before a young deputy swaggered in.

"What's all the fuss for?"

"My dog needs to go outside."

The deputy looked down at Fred staring up at him, wagging his tail. He picked Fred up. "I always wanted a dog."

"That's my dog."

The deputy glared at him. "You think I'm stupid?"

"I just want to make sure he doesn't accidentally get lost."

"It won't be my fault if he runs off." The deputy left.

Pete raked a hand through his hair. *Lord, don't let anything bad happen to Fred. I love that dog. He's the best friend I have next to You. Don't let that deputy keep him.*

Pete paced his cell for half an hour before the deputy returned. Fred ran and squeezed back into the cell, then turned and barked at the deputy.

The deputy looked from Fred to Pete. "I thought I'd keep him in the front office with me for a while. I thought he'd like that, but all he did was scratch on the door to come back here."

Pete wanted to grab the guy by the collar and remind him whose dog Fred was or at the very least yell at him, but instead he said, "Thanks for taking care of my dog for me."

The deputy nodded and turned to leave.

"One more thing."

The deputy turned back.

"Could I get some paper and a pencil?"

The deputy shrugged and nodded before leaving.

Pete waited for over two hours before anyone returned. The sheriff strolled back to his cell at the end of the row and handed him two sheets of paper and a pencil. "Otis said you wanted these."

Pete walked over to the bars and took them. "What's going to happen to me now?" He wasn't even going to try to claim innocence. It wouldn't do any good.

"The judge will look at your case tomorrow. Did I tell you the judge is my brother-in-law? I think you should have left town when you had the chance."

Keep your mouth shut, and don't make it worse for yourself, Pete.

"I didn't see a need to leave."

"And now?"

"I don't think I'll have a choice."

The sheriff gave him a smug smile and walked away.

Pete climbed back onto the wiry cot and touched the pencil tip to paper just as the single bulb that hung bare in the corridor went out. The only light.

"Sweet dreams," the sheriff called before latching the door at the end of the corridor.

Pete thumped his head back against the cement wall. The sheriff had waited to give him the paper on purpose so he couldn't write anything. He threw the pencil across his cell and heard it hit the bars before falling to the floor. The letter to Lizzie would just have to wait until morning.

In the morning, Pete rose with the first faint signs of sunrise. There was a small window in the door at his end of the corridor. The door led out to a small, walled-in exercise yard, maybe six feet by fifteen feet. That didn't matter. What was important was that he would soon have enough light to find the pencil and write a note to Lizzie.

As sunrise grew closer and light slowly illuminated his cell, Pete squinted to locate the pencil. He couldn't find it anywhere. Maybe it had rolled back under the cot, but it wasn't there, either. While he was on his hands and knees, he looked back the other way and spotted the pencil in the corridor outside his cell. Reaching through the bars, he strained to touch it but was still several inches from it.

"Fred, come here."

Fred stretched and crawled off the cot and over to him.

He pointed through the bars. "Get the pencil, Fred."

Fred squeezed through the bars and sat, staring at him.

Pete reached through. "Get the pencil."

Fred went over and sniffed the pencil.

"That's it. Pick it up and bring it to me."

Fred came back over and licked his face.

"No, get the pencil. Please."

Fred wagged his tail, barked, then went to the end of the corridor and whined to be let out.

Pete rolled onto his back on the floor. After a few minutes of feeling sorry for himself, he rose and called out, "Is anybody there?" He called out for several minutes to no avail. "It doesn't look like anyone is coming. Come on back."

Fred stayed where he was and looked from the door to Pete, back and forth, and whined.

"I'm sorry, boy. I can't help you." Pete sat back on the cot.

About ten minutes later, the door opened and Fred ran out.

"Hey, get back here," the sheriff growled.

"He needs to go outside."

"Take that rat outside and leave him there."

"That's my dog."

The single bulb glowed to life. "I can't waste my men waiting on a mutt."

Pete bit his tongue. Fred would be fine on his own for the day. Maybe he could talk the night deputy into letting Fred back in with him.

As the sheriff walked over, Pete wanted to ask him to hand him the pencil but didn't want to give the man the satisfaction of turning him down.

The sheriff stepped up to the cell, then looked down and picked up the pencil. He smiled at the pencil before handing it to Pete. "I think you dropped something."

Pete noted the broken lead. Should he bother to ask to have it sharpened? The sheriff looked from the pencil to him and waited. Pete sized him up and shoved the pencil into his pocket. "What can I do for you, sir?"

"Just checking on my prisoner." He left.

Pete pulled out the pencil and stared at the broken tip. What did he do now? He didn't have his pocketknife to whittle it sharp again. What else could he use? He looked around his cell and smiled. His cell. He went over to the cement wall and began rubbing the end at an angle on the rough surface, careful to not hurt the forming lead tip. When he had enough to write with, he sat down with the paper.

Dear Lizzie,

    Please don't believe I'm guilty, because I'm not. I don't know how that bootleg whiskey got in Jenny. I'm sure overnight, doubts have crept into your mind, but I am innocent. Please believe that. If you would only come to see me, you would know that I'm telling the truth. I think I could always tell my fact from fiction.

    Please come. I can't wait to see you.

    I love you.

Love,
Pete

A little while later, a different deputy from the one the night before came in with a plate of food. "Scrambled eggs, toast, and coffee." He set the plate on the ground and slid it under the bars through the slot.

"Deputy, I was wondering if my dog could come back in." Pete was getting lonesome.

"Sheriff doesn't want it inside."

Pete held out the note he'd written. "Could you see that Lizzie Carter gets this?"

The deputy squinted at him a moment, then nodded. "You mean Elizabeth." He took it and left.

Pete knew that the deputy would likely read it, but he just had to pretend he wouldn't. It was more important that Lizzie read it whether or not everyone else had read it, too.

          ॐ

When Lizzie pulled up in the Tin Lizzie to the post office to let Daddy out, she said, "Daddy, I know you need to be here, but would you come to the jail with me?"

Daddy patted her hand. "I think it's best if you don't go there."

She suspected Daddy was only pretending to be mildly supportive. He didn't care what happened to Pete as long as he was out of her life. "I have to see him."

"And I have to get to work. I have a family to provide for."

"But what if Sheriff Sherman won't let me see him?"

"Then there will be nothing I can say to persuade him. Go home and forget about that boy. Thaddeus Tinker was in here the other day asking about you."

Thaddeus Tinker was ten years older than she, balding, and looked like he was ready to give birth to a twenty-pound baby. "No, thank you. I'll see you later."

She drove up to the courthouse that had the jail in the basement and parked. Fred sat on the steps by the door, stood, and wagged his tail when he saw her. She picked him up. "Why are you out here?"

Fred licked her chin.

She walked inside. "Hello, Anthony. I'd like to see Lieutenant Pete Garfield."

Deputy Anthony Elmer folded a piece of paper and tucked it inside a desk drawer, then stood and straightened his uniform. "Miss Carter, it's so good to see you."

Anthony had been two grades ahead of her in school and had always been sweet on her, but she wasn't going to use that to get her way. "I brought fresh-baked muffins for Lieutenant Garfield."

Anthony swaggered around the desk and looked down at her. "He's already had breakfast."

"I'll bet he's still hungry. Can I take them to him?"

"Sheriff said not to let you see the prisoner while he was out. You can leave them here."

She wasn't going to give up that easily. "Well, the sheriff isn't here. It won't hurt to see the lieutenant for just a minute."

"I'm sorry. Sheriff's orders." Anthony was being stubborn.

"Can you at least give him his dog? Fred misses his master." She held up one of Fred's paws and waved it at Anthony.

Anthony smiled. "Sheriff doesn't want the dog in here."

What did the sheriff have against her? Or was it Pete he had issues with? But why? Pete hadn't come into town much while he was here. He couldn't have possibly caused any trouble. Did Sheriff Sherman just dislike all flyboys? "Would you tell Lieutenant Garfield I was here to see him when you give him the muffins?" At least Pete would know she'd come to visit.

On the way out of town, Lizzie stopped in at Bill's and told him and her grandpa what had happened. "Grandpa, would you go see Pete and tell him I believe he's innocent?"

Grandpa patted her hand. "Of course, darling."

"Bill, can Fred stay with you? They won't let Fred in the building with Pete."

"Sure. But he's not going to want to stay when he knows where his master is." Bill grabbed a rope. "I'll have to tie him up." He looped the rope around Fred's neck and tied the other end to a post in the garage.

As Lizzie walked out to the Ford with Finn, Fred followed her as far as he could, then barked at her. When she turned back to look at him, he wagged his tail at her. "I'm sorry. You can't come."

Fred whined and barked some more. She ignored him, got in, and started the Model T, then took one last look at Fred, who had lay down with his head on his paws, looking forlorn. Poor Fred. She sighed, then drove away.

Grandpa Finn climbed out at the courthouse. "You stay here." He came back a few minutes later, shaking his head. "They won't let anyone see the boy."

"What am I going to do?"

"Nothing you can do. When the people with the power shut you out, there's not much you can do."

Grandpa sounded like he was speaking from experience. But she couldn't just do nothing. What could she do?

❧

After lunch, Pete wasn't happy to see the sheriff again. He'd rather be lonely.

The sheriff studied him for a minute. "I sent a telegram to Spokane. The authorities said to hold you; that they would be sending someone. Looks like you've been in trouble before." The sheriff turned on his heels and walked out.

Pete bet the sheriff loved giving him that bit of news and rubbed his face. Not Spokane. Maybe he could avoid certain trouble there. He shook his head. It was all connected. She would know.

Lizzie, where are you?

Lord, please don't let her believe these lies.

He'd finally found a doll he cared about, and she was being torn from him. *Believe in me, Lizzie, believe in me.*

After a supper of cold stew and a hard biscuit, the sheriff paid him another visit. Sheriff Sherman sported a huge smile and set a chair outside his cell. If the sheriff was this happy, it couldn't be good for Pete.

"You have a visitor. A lady."

"Lizzie," he whispered. Finally she'd come. He stepped up to the bars.

"Come on in, ma'am," the sheriff called toward the door.

But instead of Lizzie, a pregnant Agatha rushed in with her three-year-old daughter. Agatha clutched the bars. "Pete, darling, are you all right? I've been so worried about you."

Pete stepped back. "What are you doing here?"

"When I heard you were in jail, I had to come." Agatha had her blond hair bobbed and wore an expensive, beaded pink dress.

Pete would rather look at the sheriff than this woman. "I don't want to see this visitor."

Agatha pushed her daughter forward. "Ruth, say hi to Daddy."

"Hi, Daddy."

The sheriff smiled and left, closing the door behind him.

"You know as well as I do that I'm not her father." Because Agatha's father was a powerful judge, she thought she could manipulate everyone. "And I'm not the father of the one you're carrying either."

"Everyone back home thinks you are." Agatha sat in the chair and fluffed her pink dress.

"Because you told them so."

"Tell Daddy you love him." Agatha pushed Ruth forward.

"I love you, Daddy." The little girl gazed up at him.

He glared at Agatha, then knelt down on the hard cement on his side of the bars. "Sweetheart, I'm not your daddy."

Ruth smiled. "Okay." She was a cute kid and deserved a better mother than Agatha. She'd probably grow up to be just like her mom.

He stood. "Why are you here, Agatha?"

"To bring you home. It's time you owned up to your responsibilities and married Ruth's mommy."

He gritted his teeth. "She's not my responsibility. And I'm not going anywhere with you."

She smiled smugly. "The three officers who came with me say otherwise."

"You can't force me to marry you."

Her features hardened. "I'm not having another child out of wedlock."

He hardened his voice. "Then marry the real father."

"You are the real father. We'll be taking the first train in the morning." Agatha took Ruth's hand. "Tell Daddy bye-bye."

"Bye-bye, Daddy."

After they left, he raked his hands through his hair. Lizzie. What would she think? *Lord, please don't let Lizzie hear about this. Keep this from her.*

He sharpened the pencil on the wall and sat down on the floor with the other sheet of paper.

My dearest Lizzie,
  I wish I could see you before I leave, but I have to go to

Spokane to take care of some business. I will come back for you.

He wanted to tell her all about Agatha, but on the slim chance no one told her, he didn't want to worry her with this. He would explain everything to her when he could see her face-to-face. Besides, he couldn't tell her in a letter and possibly make her understand. *"I love you and only you,"* he wrote, then signed the letter, *"Love, Pete."*

❧

Lizzie parked around the corner of the courthouse. Maybe the night deputy would be more sympathetic. When she approached the steps, the sheriff opened the door and held it for a young woman and her small daughter. She ducked back around the side of the building. The sheriff would never let her see Pete. He spoke with the woman for a few minutes, helped her into a taxi, and went back inside. Half an hour passed before the sheriff left and she could slip inside.

"Danny, can I see Pete Garfield?"

"My orders are to not let anyone in to see him. Only the sheriff can take people back to see the prisoner."

"Please don't call him that."

"What am I supposed to call him?"

"Pete. That's his name. And what harm could it do to let me see him for just a minute? You can be right there."

He wouldn't budge.

❧

The following morning after dropping off Daddy at work, Lizzie headed straight over to the courthouse with fresh-baked apple bread. "Hi, Anthony."

"Hello, Elizabeth. No, you can't see the prisoner."

She smiled coyly at him and sat on the edge of the desk. "Were those muffins I brought yesterday any good? Ivan said they were a bit dry."

"They weren't dry at all."

As she thought, Pete hadn't seen a one. "I brought you some apple spice bread." She unwrapped the loaf and handed him a slice.

He bit into it. "Mmm."

"Elizabeth Carter, fancy seeing you here."

Lizzie spun around to the sheriff. Rats. She'd never talk Anthony into letting her in now. "Sheriff. I'm glad you're here. I wanted to ask you if I could go downstairs."

"Of course you can. I'll take you myself."

"Really?" This was a change.

"There's no reason not to." He escorted her through the doorway and down the stairs, then unlocked the door to the cell room.

"Thank you." She stepped inside and looked at the row of four cells. All empty. She walked along the corridor to get a better look. "Where's Lieutenant Garfield?"

"Gone back to Spokane with his wife and child."

"What?"

"She's a pretty little thing, and the little girl looks just like her daddy."

"No, it can't be." Pete wasn't married.

"I saw her with my own eyes. She came last night."

Lizzie had probably seen her, too. That must be who the sheriff was letting out of the building last night. *Oh no, please don't let it be true.* Was Pete lying to her the whole time? She ran past the sheriff and up the stairs. She could hear the sheriff's laughter chase her all the way up.

She drove to Johnson's field. Pete's aeroplane was gone.

ten

Pete sat across from Agatha and Ruth on the train with two of the officers close at hand. He didn't know which bothered him more: returning to Spokane with Agatha or that cocky police officer flying his Jenny. He would be glad to have it in Spokane, but why couldn't he have flown it there? He'd offered to have one of the officers fly with him.

Agatha whispered in Ruth's ear, and the child left her seat and climbed up onto his lap, wrapped her little arms around his neck, and gave him a kiss on the cheek.

Just like her mother, throwing around her love to the wrong man. Ruth deserved to know who her real father was even if he didn't deserve her. He lifted the girl to the floor. "Go sit by your mommy." He didn't want this little one any more confused than she already was.

He was grateful for one thing: Agatha had flirted with the two officers until they agreed to unbind his wrists. She didn't want her daughter to see her "daddy" shackled. He'd promised not to try to escape. He actually wanted to go back if it meant he could clear his name and have a chance with Lizzie.

It was strange how quickly his feelings for Lizzie had rooted deep and strong after being arrested and sitting in jail. He'd had time to think about life without Lizzie. He actually never thought about the future. He took life one day at a time. There was no past and no future. Just right now. Then he met Lizzie, who cared more about his Jenny than about him. His put-on charm didn't work on her. She was different and exciting. She charged something deep inside him with her enthusiasm for flying. She'd taken hold of his heart from that first time she sat in his pilot seat. Bold, beautiful Lizzie. Now he could see the future, and it was nothing, empty, without Lizzie.

He gazed at Ruth and imagined she was his own little girl sitting next to her mommy but her mommy was Lizzie. He smiled at that picture. He'd only known Lizzie for a little more than two weeks, but for some strange reason, he was sure about her being the right doll for him. He wondered if she felt the same. She'd said she loved him, but how deep did it go? Would her love for him weather this storm?

"What are you smiling about?"

He focused on Agatha, who was smiling back at him, then turned and looked out the train window. This was going to be a long trip.

❧

Lizzie lay across her bed still crying. She couldn't stop. She moved her head to find a dry spot on her pillow, but there was none. She didn't even care anymore if her cheek was on a cold, wet part.

She'd believed in Pete. Had everything he'd told her been a lie, even the "truth" he told her? Did he mean it when he'd said he loved her? Doubtful. His wife had believed him, too, when he'd confessed his love to her. They had a daughter! He'd gone back to his wife as he should and left Lizzie with a broken heart.

And the bootleg whiskey? That was probably his, too. He'd been flying alone and then wouldn't let her fly. Was it there, and had he been trying to keep her from seeing it?

How could she have felt so much for someone in two short weeks? She thought it was one of those "it was meant to be" things, but it obviously wasn't.

*Lord, thank You for taking. . .*she sniffled. *. .him away before. . .* she choked back fresh tears. *. . .it was too late.* But she knew it was already too late. She'd fallen in love. *Take this unbearable ache away. Why did You let this happen? I wish You'd never brought Pete into my life.* It was best if she started right now to forget she'd ever met Lieutenant Pete Garfield. A new wave of sobs crashed over her, and she buried her head in her pillow. She'd never marry anyone.

She heard a knock on her door. "I'm not here." She sniffled.

"That's why you're talking to me?" Ivan said.

"Go away." She didn't want to see or talk to anyone.

"Lizzie?" Ivan's voice was clear instead of muffled by the door. He'd come in against her wishes.

"I said go away." She buried her head deeper into her cold, wet pillow.

The bed sank on the end. Ivan had obviously sat. "I'm sorry about Pete."

She nodded into her pillow.

"The sheriff was by earlier. He was telling Dad about Pete's wife and Pete leaving town with her."

She sat up quickly and glared at him. "I don't want to hear about it! Don't ever mention his name again! Ever! Do you hear me?"

Ivan's eyes had never been so wide.

"Go on now. Get out of here."

Ivan didn't move. "The sheriff said something else."

"I don't care. Just leave me be," she said through gritted teeth.

"I think the sheriff had something to do with that whiskey jug in Pe—the aeroplane."

She relaxed her jaw. "What?"

"Dad, too."

"That can't be. You misunderstood."

"The sheriff said he'd gotten rid of 'that bum, no-good flyboy.' Then he told Dad about Pete's wife and daughter and them all leaving for Spokane. Dad was pleased to hear it. Dad said he was glad Pete was finally gone. That he was nothing but trouble."

"That doesn't mean the whiskey wasn't Pete's. If anything, it proves it was. He's a liar."

Ivan shook his head. "Sheriff said it all worked better than they planned. Dad's idea of the whiskey was brilliant, but when the sheriff uncovered Pete's wife, he knew that was the nail in Pete's coffin. They could get rid of Pete and not have to deal with trying to persuade him to leave town to avoid the charges. But this way you wouldn't want to talk to Pete even if he did decide to return."

The sheriff was right about that. "They wouldn't have just told you all of this."

"They didn't know I was there. They were talking on the porch; I was inside in Dad's chair under the window. It was open a crack."

She'd been the one to open it. "I can't believe Daddy would be part of setting up Pete."

"You know how Dad is always talking about how much he needs you and if it weren't for you he couldn't do anything. I think he was afraid of Pete taking you away."

Daddy had acted like he knew nothing about the whiskey and been there for her and even gone to the sheriff for her. He'd been against her the whole time? He'd done this? She didn't want to believe Daddy would hurt her like this.

She rose, wiped her nose, and strode out to the sitting room where Daddy read his newspaper. "Is it true, Daddy?"

He looked up.

"Did you have someone put a jug of bootleg in Pete's aeroplane so the sheriff could arrest him?"

Daddy's gaze flickered from her to Ivan and back. "I think you're overwrought and dreaming things up."

She shook her head. "No. You, my loving father, wouldn't do that. You would have just asked your best friend the sheriff to run Pete out of town. Didn't you, Daddy?"

"What does it matter how it happened? The man was a liar and was using you. He's married and has a child with another one on the way. It's best you found out now."

"Daddy, how could you?"

"I'm just looking out for what's best for you. And I obviously did know what's best. You can't trust a man who has no roots and flies all over the country taking people's hard-earned money. It doesn't matter what I did. The man has a wife and child. You should be grateful and just forget about him."

Her heart would never forget Pete. He'd given her her first taste of flight. He'd let her pilot his Jenny. He'd shown her a world beyond the earth.

She stared at Daddy. Grateful? How could he have betrayed her like this? She ran outside and kept running until she was in town at Bill's Garage. She was shaking from both the fatigue of running and the growing cold. Bill and her grandpa rushed out to her.

Grandpa pulled off his outer shirt and wrapped it around her. "Come inside."

Bill looked around. "Where's your Tin Lizzie? Did it break down?"

She shook her head. "I ran."

Grandpa led her to a chair. "What happened to you?"

"Daddy." She put her face in her hands and started crying again.

"Did something happen to him? Should we call for the doctor?" Grandpa asked.

She shook her head, then spewed out the whole wretched story.

Grandpa snarled. "He don't deserve you. How that son of mine could raise a fine daughter like you, I'll never know. You must have gotten a lot of good from your ma."

Not her mom. "I doubt that. She ran off with another man."

"Then your Grandma Lilly. She was good."

❧

As the train pulled into the Spokane station, Officer Dale held out a pair of handcuffs. "Hold out your hands."

Pete did as instructed.

Agatha pushed Ruth toward him. Ruth flung her tiny arms around his neck. "Don't hurt my daddy."

He looked at Agatha and shook his head. He hated the way she used her daughter.

Agatha turned a shining smile on the two officers. "Can you give us a moment?"

Officer Dale nodded and looked to his partner. "You stay where you can keep an eye on him. I'll go see if our transportation is here."

Pete sent Ruth back to her mother.

Agatha slid forward in her seat. "All you have to do is marry me, and you won't have to spend one more minute in jail."

He leaned forward and said, "I would rather rot in jail than spend one minute married to a manipulative cat like you." He stood and held out his hands. "Officer, I'm ready to go."

Agatha stood and whispered, "Have it your way, Pete. But I think a few nights in jail will make you a little more willing." She took Ruth's hand and sashayed away.

Pete stepped off the train. He was back. It felt as though a hot coal burned in the pit of his stomach.

❧

Not more than a half hour after the jail door had swung shut, a guard came to Pete's cell. "You have a lady visitor."

He shook his head. Did Agatha think he'd changed his mind already? "I don't want to see her."

"Well, that's a fine how-do-you-do."

Aunt Ethel. He sighed. She was a sight for sore eyes even if she did look like a floozy with her bleached, bobbed hair, bright red lips, and short blue flapper dress.

He pushed off the cot and came to the bars. "It sure is good to see you."

"Of course it is." Aunt Ethel turned to the young guard. "Now be a peach and unlock this cage."

"I'm not supposed to, ma'am."

Aunt Ethel stepped closer, flashed her smile, and with a well-placed hand on the guard's chest said, "Sure you can. You have all those keys right on your belt. I'd really appreciate it."

The guard swallowed hard. "I. . .I. . .I. . ."

Pete reached through the bars and took his aunt's arm. "He can't. It's all right."

Aunt Ethel took her hand from the man's chest and let it hang by her side. "Well, go on."

"I can bring you a chair, ma'am," the guard offered.

"I don't want a chair. If you can't get my nephew the war hero out of jail, you're no use to me."

The guard hurried away.

Aunt Ethel turned a maternal face to him. "How's my little Petey?"

"I'm fine." Aunt Ethel always was his champion. She'd walk through fire for him.

"I'm going to get you out of here. I just have to find the right man in this place." She undid the top button of her dress and pulled the neckline down over the top of her shoulders.

Pete took her hand. "I appreciate what you want to do for me. But don't. I want to take care of this my own way without that kind of help."

Aunt Ethel pushed out a pouty bottom red lip.

"Promise me you won't flirt with every man in this building on my behalf." He didn't want his aunt compromising herself to help him. The Lord had a better way.

She straightened up. "Very well. But you can't expect me to just sit around and do nothing while you're stuck in here."

He smiled. "I love you, Aunt Ethel."

"I love you, too, my little Petey."

He rubbed the back of his neck. "You know I'm innocent, don't you?"

Aunt Ethel looked insulted. "Of course I do."

"I mean about everything. It's important to me that you believe I'm not the father of Agatha Marshall's daughter or of the one she's carrying."

Her expression softened. "Sure I do."

"Really?"

"Here's the way I figure it. First of all, Agatha Marshall is not the type of girl you'd like in the first place. She's manipulative and mean. Second, let's say you were blinded by love or something foolish like that and you did like her. You wouldn't get her pregnant. You're not like that. Third, if you did get a girl pregnant—which I know you never would—you would own up to it and marry her. And fourth, well, I don't know what that is, but all this is a lot of fiction. You are no more the father of her children than I am."

"Thank you." Aunt Ethel's belief in him meant more than almost anything on earth to him.

Aunt Ethel put her hands through the bars and on each of his cheeks. "How did you turn out so good with only someone like me to raise you?"

"You're not so bad. You made me go to Sunday school."

"Maybe the only thing I ever did right in my life."

"You loved me when no one else would." By most people's standards, his aunt was a disreputable floozy, but he knew she had a heart of gold. When people could get past her outward appearance—even respectable people—they loved her.

Tears pooled in his aunt's eyes. "I just can't stand to see you in here."

"Please don't do anything." He feared she'd flirt with every man in town until she got her way.

She blinked back the moisture. "Merle has a friend who's a lawyer. He'll get you out of here. I'll talk to him."

"Don't you talk to Merle's friend. I'll figure something out."

She giggled. "I'm not going to talk to him, I'm going to talk to Merle. He'll do anything for me."

Merle always was crazy for his aunt. "How is Merle?"

"Dandy and as handsome as ever."

"Has he talked you into marrying him yet?"

"Marriage would only ruin what we have."

He never understood how his aunt could live with a man she loved and who loved her more than the sun and moon and would marry her if she would ever say yes. "He loves you so much."

"The minute a man marries, he goes looking elsewhere for a younger woman. I don't want to lose him."

"Merle would never do that. He's too crazy for you. I think his heart breaks a little every day he's not married to you."

Aunt Ethel reached through the bars and caressed his cheek. "I think you've fallen in love, too. Who is she?"

He knew his aunt was uncomfortable with the subject of marrying Merle, so he allowed the change and the chance to talk about Lizzie. "I can't begin to describe how wonderful Lizzie is. She's sweet and kind. You should have heard her when I let her fly my aeroplane. She was so excited."

"You mean you gave her a ride."

"No. I let her pilot Jenny. She's even building her own aeroplane. It's a Bleriot. I was helping her wrap it in cotton."

"My, oh my. You really are in love with her."

"I've never met anyone like her and never will again."

"Does she know about Agatha?"

He nodded and the ache for Lizzie to know the truth throbbed inside him. "Agatha came with her daughter. She kept making Ruth call me Daddy. That poor little girl."

"Did Lizzie believe you when you told her the child wasn't yours?"

"I didn't get to speak to her. But as soon as all of this is taken care of, I'm going back. I'll explain everything to her."

Aunt Ethel took his hand in hers and patted it. "I'm going to talk to Merle. The sooner we get you out of here, the better." She turned and left.

He was grateful for his aunt's help. Especially if it involved someone else pleading on his behalf. His aunt's heart was in the right place; she just didn't have a problem with using questionable means.

eleven

Lizzie sat in a straight-backed chair with Fred on her lap and looked out the upstairs window of Bill's apartment above his garage into the black night. It reflected how she felt inside: dark, empty, and alone. Everything she'd cared about had been stripped away. No one was who he seemed to be.

She took the pins out of the back of her hair and let the lump fall down her back.

Pete was not a freewheeling gypsy flyboy without a care in the world who loved her as he'd made her believe. He was a husband and father with responsibilities and commitments that didn't involve her. Couldn't involve her. Had he been running away from his responsibilities?

She finger-combed her hair back and held it at the nape of her neck.

Daddy's betrayal hurt worse. He was supposed to love her no matter what. She knew he was needy and played on her sympathies because of his infirmity. He made sure she knew he "needed" her, couldn't live without her. But she never thought he'd sabotage her.

She reached toward the windowsill and picked up the scissors she'd asked Bill for.

And flying? She didn't care if she ever went up again. What was the point? It was best if she kept both feet firmly planted on the ground. Flights of fancy. Daddy had been right. Nothing good could come of flying. Her dreams had soared and taken her heart right along with them. Then they'd crashed. Just like Lincoln Beachey, grandmaster of aerial stunts and the greatest daredevil of them all. For all the wonder and spectacular flying, he was dead, smashed into the ground, and so were her dreams and her heart.

She reached behind her head and worked the scissors up and down until she'd cut through the whole wad of hair. Then she trimmed the longer front pieces to her jaw to match the length in the back. She wound the long tresses she'd cut off and folded them up in a handkerchief.

She saw headlights heading toward the garage. "Bill, you have a customer."

Bill stood from the table where he'd been playing cards with her grandpa. He looked out the window. "I think that's for you."

She took another look. Sure enough, Daddy sat in the passenger seat. But who was driving? Ivan? He came to a jerky stop.

Grandpa patted her arm. "You can stay here if you want. We'll go down and talk to him."

She followed Bill and Grandpa downstairs and to the front door with Fred in her arms but stayed back.

Grandpa did his best to straighten his old body. "She's staying here."

Daddy leaned on the open door of the Ford. "You had your chance to be a father and threw it away. I'm her father, and I know what is best for her. Come on, Elizabeth, let's go home."

"You sound just like your ma's father. He thought he knew what was best for Lilly. She died sad and lonely because of him, and he raised you to be a bitter man."

Daddy stepped away from the Ford and took a couple of steps toward Grandpa. "My grandfather was a good man. At least he was there to raise me, which is more than I can say for you."

Grandpa advanced a couple of steps. "Robert was a controlling man who didn't care about his daughter's happiness. He trained you well. You're making Lizzie just as unhappy as Robert made Lilly."

Daddy moved forward, and the two men were nearly toe-to-toe. "Her name is Elizabeth, and I think I know what's right for my own daughter."

Grandpa raised his voice. "You're only thinking of yourself."

"You're one to talk!" They were shouting at each other now.

She couldn't stand it and handed Fred to Bill. "Stop it! Both of you!" She didn't know what else to do or where to go so she walked around the Model T to get in.

Ivan looked proud behind the wheel. She could see him reaching for the door handle. She walked past the driver's door and climbed into the back.

Ivan turned in the seat. "Aren't you going to drive?"

"You drove here. You can drive us home."

Home. She didn't want to go. She didn't want to stay, either. She didn't want to do anything.

Ivan turned to her in the backseat. "But I'm not old—"

"Oh, who cares?" The sheriff certainly wouldn't do anything about it. She leaned her head against the side and stared out the window.

She felt the Ford rock as Daddy got in and shut the door. Ivan started the motor and drove off jerkily all the way home.

"What happened to your hair?" Daddy said.

She didn't want to talk to him. He could see perfectly well what happened.

"It looks awful."

Good.

Before Ivan brought the Ford to a complete stop, Lizzie jumped out and ran inside the house and locked herself in her room. Soon there was a knock on the door. It was Daddy. She'd heard his distinct walk with the thump of his wooden leg. She couldn't face him or talk to him right now, so she ignored him. Soon, he went away. He'd gotten what he wanted. She was back home.

She tossed and turned most of the night and finally fell

into a fitful sleep in the early morning hours. A knock on her door woke her. She donned her housecoat and answered it, barely able to open her eyes.

Ivan stared at her. "Daddy's ready to leave for work."

"I can't go. You drive him."

"But...but..."

"But he's going to be late. Go."

Ivan ran off down the hall. She crawled back into bed and soon heard the Ford start up and drive away, then drifted back to sleep.

❧

First thing that same morning, Merle and his friend Timothy showed up at Pete's cell. Merle looked distinguished as ever in a three-piece suit and sporting a full, well-trimmed beard and mustache. Something Pete could never pull off.

Timothy looked to be about Merle's age, in his upper forties. He adjusted his spectacles. "I'll be honest. It doesn't look good. They are trying to pin the murder of old man Sutton on you. You weren't even in town. Seems they are saying you flew back into town during the dark of night to kill the old man for no apparent reason and left again."

Pete raked a hand through his hair. "This is Agatha's doing. She's trying to get me to agree to marry her." He told Timothy the whole history with Agatha.

"So the man she was going to marry four years ago is the father of her children. Why doesn't she try to get him to marry her?"

"He's not the father, either." Pete would not divulge who the real father was.

"Do you know who the father is?"

"I won't say."

Timothy frowned. "It would help you an awful lot if we could expose her whole torrid affair."

He wouldn't do that. "Too many people would be hurt."

Timothy's voice rose. "People need to take responsibility for their actions, not you."

"I won't do it."

Timothy shook his head. "He's not making this easy on me, Merle. I'll see what I can do, but you talk some sense into him." He walked away.

Merle had remained quiet until now. "I'm proud of you." He stuck his hand through the bars and shook Pete's hand. "You are the son I never had, and I couldn't be more proud if you were my own flesh and blood."

Pete's eyes stung. He was a grown man. How could he feel like crying? Merle had always treated him like family. "I never told you how much I've appreciated everything you've done for my aunt and me." Merle had found a job for Aunt Ethel when they were hungry and about to be thrown out onto the streets. He'd bought food and left it by their front door, though he'd never 'fessed up to it. Merle had known Aunt Ethel would insist on paying him back. He'd fallen madly in love the first time he'd met Aunt Ethel, but she was afraid of marriage and would agree only to live with Merle. Merle had refused at first, then figured maybe it would get Aunt Ethel to soften up and marry him. Fifteen years later, he was still trying to soften her up.

"About this Agatha."

"I won't rat her out. I can't stand her, but I won't hurt everyone else involved to get revenge on her and gain my freedom."

"The real father means something to you?"

He shook his head. "It's someone else who would be hurt by all this. I would rather be the one he hates." Pete's best friend, David, had felt betrayed by him and refused to believe Pete wasn't the father of his ex-fiancée's child. David had rejected both Pete and Agatha. Agatha had tried to get David to move up the wedding so she could pass off another man's child as his. When that hadn't worked, she'd tried to seduce David. And when that hadn't worked and she had begun to show and David had turned her away, she had pointed her finger at Pete. Why Pete? Because he knew who the likely real father was. "I feel like Shadrach, Meshach, and Abednego thrown into the fiery furnace. I may survive this or not, but God is still in control. And for the first time in my life, I'm trusting Him to do His will, whatever that is."

Merle nodded. "Timothy doesn't understand your honor. I'll explain to him that you can't, in good conscience, betray this confidence."

"Thank you."

Merle looked to the ground, then back up at him. "He may not be able to help you."

"I understand. I'm trusting God to make this all work out. And Merle, don't let Aunt Ethel do anything foolish to try to secure my freedom."

"That's a tall order, boy. I'll do my best."

Pete had the utmost confidence in Merle and could rest easier knowing Merle was looking out for his aunt.

❧

Lizzie stayed in bed all that day, thinking and crying about Pete when she wasn't sleeping. She'd given herself this one day to mourn. Tomorrow she'd go to the warehouse and start packing apples like the rest of the girls had done last week when she was helping Pete. And next week she'd begin rolling chewy Aplet candies in powdered sugar as the season started into full swing.

She got up long enough to make supper but didn't bother to change out of her nightclothes to do the task. She peered out the kitchen window and saw Ivan motoring wildly up the road. He needed to learn to make smaller adjustments. When they came to a stop at the house, she went back to her room.

This was her time, and she would not allow Daddy in it.

Awhile later, she heard an automobile and looked out her bedroom window but couldn't see who it was. Still in her heavy flannel nightgown and housecoat, she shimmied out the window and tiptoed across the cold ground around the corner of the house. Bill and Grandpa stood next to Bill's old truck. Daddy came out onto the porch.

Grandpa stepped forward holding up some papers. "Robert filled your head with a bunch of lies."

"You expect me to believe a man who wouldn't even own up to his own responsibilities?"

"That's not true. I loved your mother, and we were married. Robert dissolved our marriage because he didn't approve of me."

Daddy shook his head. "Go away, old man." He went back inside.

Lizzie came around the corner. "What are those?"

"Letters from Lilly."

"May I take them? I'll bring them back tomorrow."

Grandpa stared at the two letters, then reluctantly handed them over. "It's all I have from her."

She hugged them to her chest. "I'll take good care of them." She crawled back up to her window, clambered into the room, and sat on her bed.

The letters were well worn and nearly falling apart. She unfolded the first one carefully: "*My Dearest Cullen, I'm so torn. I love you bo—*"

The words in the fold were worn away. BO? What word could that be? Boy? That didn't make sense. The next word only had the last four letters *ther*. Mother? Father? Brother? Peter?

She knew it couldn't be Pete but stopped and pictured his carefree smile and the way he'd looked at her when he'd refused her repeated requests to fly his Curtiss JN-4D. That's the Pete she'd fallen in love with. She didn't want to think about the Pete he really was.

She read on: "*—ther is being so unreasonable. I promise to get him to accept you.*"

Him. So *ther* must be father. She went back to the beginning.

"*I'm so torn. I love you. . .both.*" It must be. "*Father is being so unreasonable. I promise to get him to accept you before*"—something, then—"*aby comes.*" It must be *the baby comes.*

"*Don't give up my love. Your faithful and loving wife, Mrs. Cullen Finnegan.*"

Her great-grandparents had been married. Lizzie had gotten the impression from Daddy that they weren't.

She set the letter aside and gently unfolded the other one. It was in as bad shape as the other. She took the letters to her writing desk, pulled out clean paper, and began copying what she could make out, then read the letter for meaning and content and was able to fill in all the blanks. She wasn't sure if it was exactly right, but it all made sense:

My Dearest Cullen,

   Father is still unmoving. I have promised him that I will steal away with you. I shouldn't have told him. He watches me always. And locks me in my room! I'm not a child! I am going to pretend I am content after the baby comes. Pretend I have forgotten about you. He will let down his guard, and I will run away with our baby. I'll meet you in our special place on our first anniversary. Come to me, my love.

Your faithful and loving wife,
Mrs. Cullen Finnegan

Lizzie copied the first letter. Then she made a second copy of both for herself.

So legally, she was Elizabeth Finnegan. Lizzie Finnegan. She liked that. She might have been Lizzie Garfield. She shook her head. Even if Pete hadn't been married and had a family, he never would have settled down. He was a flying gypsy, never staying anyplace very long. And she was rooted in place by Daddy.

❧

A jail guard opened the door separating the cells from the rest of the world. "You're a popular boy. You have another visitor."

Pete's jaw unhinged when he saw his best friend approach. David had sworn never to talk to him again. He rose from the cot, walked cautiously across the cell, and waited for David to speak first.

"I can't say I'm disappointed to see you behind bars. Just tell me why? Why my girl when you could have had any girl you wanted?"

Pete grabbed the bars. "It wasn't me. I swear to you."

David shook his head. "I've heard your song and dance before. You know who it is but won't spill the beans. I think you're just saying that. Why wouldn't you want to tell and clear your name?"

"I have my reasons." He wanted his oldest friend to believe him just on his word.

"They say you killed old man Sutton."

He seemed to attract lies like garbage attracted flies. "I wasn't even in town. I didn't do it."

David glared at him. "You may be a cad, but you're no murderer."

Pete guessed that was something.

"I talked to Agatha. She said if you married her, she'd see to it that all the charges were dropped. If you won't do it to save your own neck, do it for your daughter and the one on the way."

Pete gritted his teeth. He'd rather have his best friend believe him about Agatha than the murder charge. "I'm not the father." How many times did he have to say it?

David shook his head. "I just came to tell you that if you won't be a man and own up to your responsibilities, then I will."

"What?"

"I'll marry her if she'll get you cleared, but then you have to leave town and never return." David pointed a condemning finger at him.

"You're going to marry Agatha? You can't. You said you'd never marry her. You said she made you sick." Pete shook the unyielding bars.

"You're the one who makes me sick now. I thought you were a better man than this. Don't you care at all about your own children?"

"For the last time, there is no way I could possibly be the father of Agatha's daughter or of the one she's carrying."

"Be honest for once in your life."

How ironic. When he was telling the truth, no one believed him. "For the friendship we once had, please don't marry her."

"The only way I won't marry her is if you own up and take care of your responsibilities."

He couldn't let his best friend ruin his life this way, not when he had the means to stop it. He could marry Agatha, or he could tell David who the real father was. If he married Agatha, then he'd have no chance of winning Lizzie's heart back and convincing her of his innocence. But if he told the truth, David would be crushed.

"If you don't leave town after we're married and you're released, I'll have you thrown back in jail." David walked away.

Pete's gut twisted, and his heart ached. "David, wait." He couldn't let his friend ruin his life.

David shook his head and kept walking.

"I'll tell you who it is." David deserved better than Agatha.

David hesitated, then came back. He folded his arms and waited without a word.

"Four years ago, I saw Agatha and a man. She was coming out of a hotel in the middle of the day with him. And they were kissing, right there in the open. She turned and saw me."

"So why didn't she point the finger at the real father? None of this makes sense."

"Because he's married."

"Married?" David clearly didn't believe him.

"It would destroy his marriage if his wife found out."

"Why would you protect a married man who is unfaithful to his wife? That makes no sense."

"He's not the one I'm protecting."

"Agatha? You should have thought of that before you got her pregnant."

"Not Agatha."

"Then who?"

"You."

"You're crazy." David turned to leave again.

"It's Saul."

David froze for a full half minute. Then he turned and said, "My brother? You want me to believe that my happily married brother would betray me and his lovely wife and have an affair with my fiancée? Is that what you expect me to believe?"

"It's the truth."

"He has a beautiful wife and three children."

"Make that four with another on the way. And a mistress."

David came at him and reached through the bars swinging at him. Pete stepped back out of reach, for once grateful for the bars. David gritted his teeth. "My brother would never do that to me. Never. He was a father to me."

"I'm sorry, David."

David pulled his arms back and straightened his coat. "I hope you rot in here." He walked away.

Pete slumped onto his cot. *Lord, let him hate me for the rest of his life, but don't let him marry Agatha. She'll ruin him more than this ever would.*

twelve

The next morning, Lizzie rose early and readied herself, then went out and prepared Daddy and Ivan's breakfast and left it on the stove to stay warm until they came out to eat. She put on her coat and went out to feed the chickens and do her other outside chores. When she'd finished, she sat in the Ford and waited on Daddy and Ivan. Neither said a word when they came out and climbed in. She let Ivan off at school and drove to the post office.

"How long are you going to refuse to speak to me, Elizabeth?"

"I prefer Lizzie." She knew Daddy hated that nickname.

"I can't bear having you mad at me."

She didn't look at him. "You hurt me more than I thought you ever could."

Daddy sat silent a moment. "I love you, Elizabeth."

She knew he did but couldn't return the words. She sat staring ahead, willing him to get out of the automobile.

He climbed out and hobbled with more effort than usual, no doubt for her benefit. She drove away and to Bill's Garage. Fred ran out with his tail wagging in circles. She picked him up. Grandpa met her at the door, and she handed him his letters. "I kept them safe." Then she handed him one set of the copies. "Some of the words are hard to make out, so I made copies so you could always read Grandma's words to you."

Grandpa put his hand on his chest. "They are all right here. I have every word memorized. I just like to look at her script."

Tears welled in her eyes. That was so sweet. "At the end of the second letter, Lilly mentioned your special place. Where is it?"

Grandpa gave a faraway smile. "Down Memory Lane."

Was that a real place? "Where's that?"

"There was an old wagon trail out by that field Pete landed in. There was a single wild rosebush alongside the ruts. Lilly said it probably greeted the new settlers to the area and was now there to greet us and usher us into our new life together. I plucked a blossom off it for her. She said she was going to press it and keep it in her Bible."

Bill stood, went upstairs, and came back down several minutes later. "I nearly forgot she gave this to me." He handed an old Bible to Grandpa. "It was Lilly's."

Bill had Grandma's Bible? That was strange. "Why do you have her Bible?"

"Lilly and I were second cousins. She asked me to hold onto it for her."

Grandpa opened the Bible and in the crack of the pages found a small, pressed wild rose. He smiled. "She kept it. I's never sure if she did." He presented the flower to Lizzie. "She would want you to have it."

Lizzie knew where the wild rosebush was. It grew on the dividing line between the Johnsons' property and the Shorts'. When she was in school, there was an old legend that an Indian maiden named Night Moon sat there waiting for her true love, Little Elk, to return to her. Little Elk drowned in the river and never came back. She cried many tears, and the bush grew to keep her company. The bush was said to be Little Elk. When Night Moon died, a black-capped chickadee sat on the bush, and the two lovers were always together. People at school believed if you got a boy to kiss you by that bush, he would marry you.

Maybe she should have taken Pete there for their first kiss.

She shook her head. It wouldn't have changed anything. Pete had been married long before she'd met him.

"What's wrong?" Grandpa asked.

"I was just thinking about Pete." She sighed. "Say, Grandpa, you knew Pete a long time. Tell me about his wife and child. How could he just leave them behind?"

Grandpa frowned. "I hadn't seen little Pete in a few years so I wouldn't know anything about a wife or nothing."

She sat by the potbellied stove with Bill and Grandpa, sharing a pot of coffee.

"Even though I think what your father did was wrong, he did you a favor. You may not have found out about Pete's wife and child until it was too late."

And when exactly was too late? She'd already fallen in love.

"Let him go. The sooner you do, the sooner you can start living again."

"How long did it take you to get over Grandma and start living again?"

Grandpa got a faraway look again. "I haven't been alive for forty-five years."

How sad.

"I never did get over Lilly. Maybe if I'd gotten to say good-bye or she had sent me away, I could have. She was the solid ground I needed to sink my roots into. Without her, I've just drifted through a meaningless existence like a dried-up leaf on the wind. I've met some nice folks along the way. But I could never stay put for long. I tried, though."

Her grandpa had had such a sad, wasted life. Would she end up like him? Always pining for her first love. She walked out to the other building. Her Bleriot sat half covered in cotton fabric. Pete had been so eager to help her. The first person she could share her dream with. She grabbed an old pair of coveralls Bill had given her and pulled them on over her dress. The skirt would get wrinkled, but she didn't care. She began covering the other wing.

❧

That evening back at home as she cleaned up after supper, Lizzie kept looking out the window until finally she saw headlights. Daddy had tried hard not to be a bother to her but had let her know how much he needed her. She opened the door and let Bill and Grandpa in before they knocked.

Daddy turned in his chair. "What's he doing here?"

"I invited him."

"Well, he's not welcome in my house." Daddy struggled to his feet and planted his wooden leg firmly on the floor.

She stood in front of Daddy. "You need to hear what he has to say. After what you did to Pete, it's the least you can do for me."

"That boy was no good and neither is he." Daddy pointed at Grandpa. "I want him out of my house."

She folded her arms. "If you throw him out before he says what he came for, then I'm leaving, too."

Daddy eyed her to see if she was telling the truth. She'd decided if he was so unyielding as to not even let Grandpa have his say, whether he believed him or not, then she didn't want to stay. Daddy frowned and sat back down.

Grandpa let Daddy read the copies of the letters from Lilly. Daddy handed them back. "Those prove nothing. Mrs. Cullen Finnegan could be anyone. Those could have been written by the barmaid at the local tavern for all I know."

Grandpa handed Daddy Lilly's Bible open to the center where the family genealogy was. "Right there." Grandpa jabbed his finger on the page. "*Cullen Andrew Finnegan and Lillian Rose Carter, Married July 8th, 1875.*" Next to the entry was written *Mrs. Cullen Finnegan* with a smiling face.

"Grandpa, do you have the originals of Grandma's letters with you?"

Grandpa pulled them out of his coat pocket and handed them to Lizzie. She opened one of the letters. "Look, the signatures are the same."

Daddy scowled.

Bill stepped forward and handed Daddy an aged check. "Finn doesn't know I still have this. Uncle Robert gave him a large check to dissolve the marriage and leave town and never speak to Lilly again."

Lizzie leaned over to see the amount. "Five thousand dollars!" That was a fortune.

"Finn never cashed it. He told me that Lilly was worth a whole lot more to him than any amount of money."

Daddy hobbled to his room with little effort and closed his door.

Grandpa went to the front door. "It's up to him now what he chooses to believe."

❧

"You've been working real hard on this contraption," Grandpa said.

Lizzie climbed out from under her aeroplane where she was painting the last of the cotton with dope. "I have to go see Pete."

"You're actually going to try to fly this thing?"

"Sure." There was no reason she shouldn't.

Grandpa shook his head. "One bad idea after another."

"It'll fly. I have to see Pete."

"That's not a good idea. He has a wife and child."

"I have to tell him that I know that jug of whiskey was put in his aeroplane by someone else and to see for myself that he has a wife. What if there was some mix-up?"

Grandpa shook his head. "Child, there was no mix-up."

"You yourself said that if you could have said good-bye or Grandma had turned you away you could have let her go. I need to go say good-bye so I can let him go. At the very least,

I have to give him his dog." She picked up Fred. Fred preferred to stay around the aeroplane. "I think he misses his master."

"You're making a mistake. Let me take his dog back to him. I'll give him an earful, too."

"Thank you, Grandpa, but this is something I have to do."

That night as Lizzie packed a small bag to take with her, Daddy came into her room.

"So you're really going to go?"

"Don't try to talk me out of it."

"I'm sorry for the trouble I've caused. I never wanted to hurt you."

She turned to face him. Did he really mean it? She could see the sorrow on his face. He held out some folded papers.

She took them. "What are these?"

"Just one more of my many mistakes. Lou gave me the first two. The other came in the mail." Tears filled his eyes. "Come back to me, please." He walked out.

She sat on the edge of her bed and unfolded the first sheet of paper:

Dear Lizzie,

   Please don't believe I'm guilty because I'm not. I don't know how that bootleg whiskey got in Jenny. I'm sure overnight, doubts have crept into your mind, but I am innocent. Please believe that. If you would only come and see me, you would know that I'm telling the truth. I think you could always tell my fact from fiction.

   Please come. I can't wait to see you.

   I love you.

Love,
Pete

Pete had written to her while he sat in jail? *I believe you.* She read the next letter:

My dearest Lizzie,
I wish I could see you before I leave, but I have to go to
Spokane to take care of some business. I will come back for you.
I love you and only you.

Love,
Pete

Business? Is that what he called his family?

She pulled the last letter out of the envelope. Daddy had opened it and obviously read it:

My Dearest Lizzie,
I was very disappointed that you did not come to see me,
but I can understand you not wanting to go to the jail.

They hadn't even told Pete that she had come, but they wouldn't let her see him. Wouldn't even give him the muffins she baked him.

You no doubt have heard about Agatha and Ruth.

Which one was his wife and which one his daughter?

I can't explain it to you in a letter. It's too complicated.
I would be at your side right now to tell you everything, but
I'm sitting in a jail here in Spokane. Again, I'm innocent.
Please, please give me a chance to explain everything.
Then if you want me to go away, I will. I don't know when
I'll get out of here, but I'll come as soon as I can.
I can't stand not seeing you and talking to you. Please wait
for me.
I love you.

All my love,
Pete, your flyboy

How could he sign it that way when he had a wife? She was probably a perfectly likable, sweet girl who believed everything Pete had promised her. Or was there a good explanation and this was all a misunderstanding? Lizzie wanted to hope for Pete but couldn't with the thought of Agatha and Ruth.

She would go and say good-bye, and let Pete live his life.

❧

Wednesday morning, Lizzie pulled up in front of the post office. "Daddy, I'll leave the Ford at Bill's Garage. Ivan can go over there and get it and take you home."

Daddy just sat staring forward.

She was not going to let him talk her out of going.

"I know I don't have a right to ask."

Be strong. Say no. "But?"

"I wanted to have him over for supper tonight."

"Him? You mean Grandpa?"

He nodded.

She sucked in a breath. "Really?" Had he accepted what Grandpa had said as the truth?

"I need you there. Will you stay one more night? I can't do this without you."

Did Daddy honestly want to reconcile with Grandpa? Or was this just an excuse to keep her here? Would there be another excuse tomorrow?

But if she could help bring Daddy and Grandpa together, how could she pass that up? She just didn't know. She could tell Daddy she would do it when she returned.

"I promise it will only be this one night."

She sighed. "Okay, but no excuses tomorrow. I will leave."

Daddy smiled at her. "Will you invite him?"

She nodded. "What would you like me to make?"

"Anything you want. Maybe you could ask him what he'd like." Daddy kissed her cheek and got out.

Please, Lord, don't let him just be doing this to delay me.

She stopped by Bill's and invited both men, though Grandpa was skeptical.

"Isn't this why you came back here, to reconcile with your son?"

"He's had years of Robert telling him I'm a bad person. I don't know if a couple of letters can overcome that."

"It's a start. He's willing to see you. I'm making your favorite supper."

Grandpa brightened. "Really?"

"Just tell me what you want."

᱾

Lizzie moved the pan of fried chicken to the side of the stove to keep warm, then looked out the kitchen window again. Where were they? Please don't let Grandpa have chickened out. Then she saw headlights in the distance. "They're coming."

Daddy got up from his chair and stood in the middle of the room, staring at the door. He jumped at the knock on the door.

She answered it, but only Bill stood on the porch. "Where's Grandpa?"

"In the truck. He says he's not coming in unless he knows for sure he's welcome."

"Of course he's welcome," she said. "I'll go talk to him." Daddy and Grandpa were too close to putting the past to rest for her to let this opportunity slip away.

"I'll go." Daddy thumped across the floor and out the door, leaving it open. He stood on the porch. "Are you going to make me risk my neck hobbling down these steps and drag you out of that old truck, old man?"

Lizzie cringed and heard a door open and shut. She hoped Grandpa didn't take offense to Daddy's gruffness.

"Is that your polite way of telling me I'm welcome in your house?"

"It's cold out here, and Elizabeth fixed a fine supper."

She smiled. It was worth staying an extra day, but she would take no excuses from Daddy tomorrow.

thirteen

Thursday morning, Lizzie pulled up to the post office and before Daddy could say anything, she spoke, "No favors and no excuses. I'm leaving today."

Daddy stared out the windshield. "There's nothing I can say to change your mind?"

She shook her head adamantly.

"I just want you to know I don't think you should do this. He's not worth your time."

"I'm doing this for Fred. He needs to be back with his owner."

Daddy put a hand on hers. "Let me buy you a train ticket then."

"I'm flying, Daddy. I'll be back, maybe even tonight."

"I hope so." Daddy took her hand and kissed it. "I love you."

"I love you, too."

He climbed out and hobbled inside.

She wanted to stay just to please him, but she knew she could never get over Pete until she went to him and said good-bye and gave back Fred. She drove to Bill's. Bill and Grandpa met her out at her aeroplane as she did a final safety check of the tires, gauges, and wires holding the wings straight.

"You're a crazy fool," Grandpa said.

"Is that your way of wishing me luck?"

"You're going to need more than luck to get that thing off the ground."

If it wouldn't fly, she'd walk. "Luck will have nothing to do with my aeroplane taking off. It will be all God's doing." She spent half the night praying the Bleriot would fly; the other half thanking God for Daddy and Grandpa forgiving each other. The meal had been a little awkward with two men set in their ways, trying to compromise without yielding.

She tossed her small overnight bag in and hoisted Fred up. She'd made him a little coat harness and tied a rope to it to keep him from jumping out. Fred put his paws up on the side of the cockpit and wagged his stubby tail vigorously, happy to be in an aeroplane again. Bill and Grandpa helped her push it out to the dirt road behind the garage. It was wide enough and long enough. . .she hoped. It was the reason she'd asked Bill if she could build her aeroplane here. There was a ready-made runway.

She hugged the two old men good-bye and climbed aboard. She put on her leather helmet and goggles, got Fred situated on her lap, and took a deep breath. The engine roared to life and her stomach flopped like a fish tossed on the riverbank. She'd never flown alone before. She'd only piloted an aeroplane twice. With Pete's help and guidance.

Lord, You're going to have to help me this time.

This was Betty's maiden voyage. She figured if Pete's aeroplane was called Jenny, hers needed a name, too.

She pushed the throttle forward and picked up speed. She came to the end of the road and gave a little scream as the wheels left the ground. Betty sailed up and over the house and orchard beyond.

"Yippee!" She was airborne. Betty felt good and solid. Not as good as Jenny had, but she was a good machine. Lizzie hoped. *Thank You, Lord.* She circled back around over the garage and waved to Bill and Grandpa. Then she flew over the town, circled back twice, and came lower over the post office as Daddy came out. She waved. When she flew over the school, the children poured out of the building. Ivan led the pack waving and jumping. She waved back then pointed Betty east.

After half an hour of flying she noticed the engine sputter, then cough. That wasn't right. She listened closely for a minute as it got worse, then choked to death. The propeller stopped.

Panic seized her.

She didn't know what to do. *Pete, what do I do?* There was no open place to land. She was going to crash and die out here, and no one would even know.

What do I do? What do I do?! Tears filled her eyes. She couldn't see and tried to wipe them away. "Help me, Lord."

She blinked several times and thought she saw a small meadow. Was it big enough to land in? If so, would she be able to take off again if she could get Betty flight ready again? There was no place else. She had to land there. For better or for worse, she was going down. Fred was hunkered way down at her side as though he knew they were in for a rough landing. Poor dog was shaking.

The aeroplane wobbled as she descended sharply. "Hold together, Betty." She did her best to steady the craft and line up for her landing. "Lord, please get us down safely and unharmed. All three of us." She had to include Betty in that prayer, or she'd never get off the ground again. She hit hard and bounced across the meadow like a wounded bird hopping around. Betty finally came to a stop.

She released a huge, captive breath. Fred raised his head. She picked him up and kissed his head. "We made it! Thank You, Lord!"

She climbed out and set Fred on the ground. "Okay, Betty, what's the problem?" She needed to get into the engine and see why it quit on her. Pete'd had it running smoothly. She couldn't imagine he overlooked something. Then she just stared at the aeroplane. She hadn't brought one single tool. Stupid, stupid, stupid. A good pilot would know better than that. Always carry tools. Pete would know that.

She'd seen a town a couple of miles back, just before the engine started acting up. She'd get tools there. She took hold of the rope tied to Fred's coat harness and headed for the railroad tracks. She hiked along the tracks for an hour before she came to the town and found the hardware store. She bought the tools she'd need and headed back.

☙

That same Thursday, a week after David's visit, Merle visited Pete with good news. All charges were dropped. Pete was a free man.

"Agatha has named another man as the father of her children and is apparently going to marry him."

"No." *David, don't do this.* "They aren't married yet?"

"I think it's set for the day after tomorrow."

Then there was still time. He would talk sense into David one way or another. Or maybe she'd given up on him and named some other poor fool. Dare he hope the real father? When Pete stepped outside, David was standing across the street. David gave him a salute and walked away. Then it was David who was going to marry Agatha.

He ran to catch up. "David!"

David turned, a sad, broken man.

"You can't marry Agatha. Don't do it."

"I can't destroy my brother's marriage. He's done so much for me." David looked so dejected.

"Then you believed me after all."

David shook his head. "I spoke to my brother. I told him your accusations. He told me it was true and begged me not to tell Julia. Then I confronted Agatha. She said if I didn't marry her, she would go straight to Julia."

"So you bartered your happiness away for your brother's and mine?"

"No less than what you tried to do for me." David shoved his hands deep into his trouser pockets.

"But I wasn't willing to marry her."

"You were willing to rot in jail."

He couldn't believe David was willing to do this. "Don't marry her."

"I don't have any other choice. She'll tell Julia." David hesitated. "You're free to stay in town if you want."

"Does that mean we're friends again?" Pete held out his hand.

David looked from his hand to his face. "You'd really be friends with me after all this?"

"I never stopped being your friend. If I had, I wouldn't have been in jail."

David shook his hand. "Thanks, Pete." Forgiveness was a sweet thing.

The police wouldn't release Jenny to Pete until tomorrow. It was getting late, anyway. The flight to Cashmere would take longer than the daylight he had left. Pete went to his aunt's apartment. Merle was there in his usual chair, smoking his pipe. He had a house but lived here because Aunt Ethel wouldn't move into his house.

"Aunt Ethel, in the jail you said you'd do anything for me."

She put her hand on his cheek. "You know I would."

"Marry Merle."

She pulled her hand away and furrowed her brow. "You know I can't do that. What if he leaves me?"

"He won't leave you. He loves you. Take a chance on love." It's what he was going to do.

"I don't know."

"Think on it."

Aunt Ethel gave a small gesture that was a cross between a shrug and a nod.

&

Once Lizzie started poking around the engine, it was easy to see the problem. Her gasoline line had holes chewed in it. A mouse must have gotten in. She pulled it off. She might be able to repair it with a little dope and fabric. It wouldn't be great, but it might get her to Spokane. First, she would check to see if that little critter did any more damage. Sure enough. The spark plug wire was chewed. She didn't know which had brought her down. She couldn't fix the wire with dope. She would have to go back into town. Why hadn't she looked for the problem before she'd gone into town the first time?

She sighed and started the trek back to the hardware store and bought a tube to replace her gasoline line, wire for the spark plug, and some crackers and jerked beef. By the time she returned, the sun was setting. There wasn't enough daylight to make the repairs, and she hadn't brought a lantern or any matches to start a fire. She hadn't expected to be spending the night out in the middle of nowhere. She hadn't brought a blanket, and the temperature was already dropping.

Pete never would have let himself get in this position. He would've had everything he needed. At least she'd strapped her tarp to the back of her seat. She could cover Betty and protect her from deer. That was more than Pete'd had.

Before she was completely out of daylight, Lizzie covered Betty with the tarp and tied it in place, then ate her small meal. She rubbed her arms from the growing cold. Now what did she do about herself? She could wrap herself in the tarp, but if any deer decided to come, she'd be in trouble tomorrow. No, Betty needed the tarp more than she did. She could sit in the cockpit and hope enough heat would be trapped in there to keep her warm, but then she'd never sleep sitting up like that.

"Fred, do you have any suggestions?"

Fred put his front paws on her leg. She picked him up and walked around Betty all snug under the tarp. Then she noticed the extra tarp at the tail. She'd tied a rope around the whole wad to keep it in place. She untied it and pulled a huge corner free and retied the rest. Perfect. She wrapped herself and Fred in the large corner and lay down to sleep.

Sleep was intermittent. Every noise drew her attention. Were deer coming to destroy her aeroplane? Or was it something more dangerous coming after her? She felt so vulnerable out in the open.

❧

The next morning while Pete sat at the kitchen table, Merle came in shaking his head.

"You look dapper this morning." Pete took a sip of his java. He'd be leaving as soon as he could get his aeroplane from the police.

"Your aunt has something up her sleeve. She told me I had to wear this suit and that we were going for a drive. Are you coming?"

"I don't think so." His aunt hadn't said anything to him.

"Of course you are." Aunt Ethel swept into the kitchen dressed in a plain pink dress that came all the way down past her knees, a string of pearls, and pale pink lip rouge. "You aren't dressed yet," she exclaimed, looking at Pete in his undershirt and trousers.

"I didn't know we had some place to be."

Aunt Ethel pulled him up by the arm. "We don't. Just get dressed. Wear that nice brown suit I always liked." She pushed him toward his room. "Hurry now."

His aunt had always acted different than other people, but this was odd even for her. Pete dressed, and when he came out of his room, she was waiting in the hall to inspect him, just like she did every Sunday morning before she dropped him off at church. "Are we going to church?"

"Shh. Don't tell Merle."

"Aunt Ethel, are you going to finally marry him?"

Aunt Ethel put her finger to her pale pink lips. "Keep your voice down."

"You're going to marry him without telling him?"

"I figure when I get to the church, if I change my mind, it won't hurt him as much if I back out." She nodded, evidently pleased with his appearance. "He's ready. Let's get in the Packard."

Merle helped Aunt Ethel in, then climbed into the driver's seat. "Where to?"

"Oh, I don't care," Aunt Ethel said in a breezy voice. "Just drive."

Merle shrugged again, started the automobile, and motored away.

"Turn left up here," Aunt Ethel said. She gave him several more directions.

Merle turned and gave Aunt Ethel a hard look. "Woman, are you sure you don't have a destination in mind?"

"No, none at all. Just a nice little drive. Aren't these nice houses on this street?"

Merle looked up the street. "Real nice. What are you up to?"

"Nothing." Aunt Ethel fidgeted with her handbag. "This was a bad idea. Let's just go home." She was chickening out.

Pete leaned forward. "Hang a right."

Merle did, and Aunt Ethel yelled, "Pull over!"

Merle parked and turned off the engine. He looked from Aunt Ethel to Pete and back, clearly wanting to know what was going on.

Pete opened his door in the back. "I'm just going to stretch my legs. How about you, Merle?"

"I'm fine."

"Oh, come on." Aunt Ethel climbed out. "Let's all stretch our legs." She seemed to be back on track with her plan.

Merle shook his head and opened his door.

Pete leaned close to his aunt and whispered, "This would go a lot easier if you told him."

"Not yet."

"Then when?"

"When the minister asks him to take his vows. I don't want him to have a chance to back out."

Pete shook his head. If he spilled the beans, his aunt might deny it and be the one to back out. . .forever. So his job was to get them both in the church as quickly as possible.

He put a hand on Merle's shoulder. "Merle, come with me, and don't ask any questions."

Merle opened his mouth, then closed it.

"Just trust me." Pete guided him inside the church.

Merle leaned toward him and said in a low voice, "I hope you're going to explain all this to me later."

Pete smiled. "I don't think I'll need to. How about you two stay here for a minute? I want to say hello to the minister. I haven't seen him in a while."

Aunt Ethel looked pale but nodded, as did Merle. Merle was a good sport. He was probably the only person, beside Pete, who could put up with Aunt Ethel's eccentricities.

Pete left the two in the hallway, hoping Aunt Ethel would tell Merle what they were all doing there, and opened the door to the minister's office. "Hello, Minister Hanson."

The short, round, and balding man behind the desk stood. "Pete, my boy, sit down."

"I don't really have the time right this moment, but do you have enough time to perform a quick marriage ceremony?"

Minister Hanson gave him a huge smile. "Sure."

"I'll be right back." Pete ducked out before the minister could question him. Merle stood alone. "Merle, where's Aunt Ethel?"

"She said she'd be right back. Will you tell me what's going on now?"

"Wait here." Pete hurried and caught up to Aunt Ethel outside. "Where are you going?"

"I can't do it." Aunt Ethel took quick, short breaths.

"You have to."

"Why?"

"Because Merle will want to know what we're doing here, and when you tell him that you chickened out on marrying him, he'll be heartbroken. He'll never look at you the same."

"What if he says no?"

He took his aunt by the arm. "He won't."

"There you are, darling." Merle gave Aunt Ethel a loving smile. "Shall we go back inside?"

"Why?" Aunt Ethel said.

Merle wrapped her free hand around his forearm. "Just a nice little walk." He winked at Pete. Minister Hanson must have told him.

They met the minister at the front of the chapel, and Merle leaned toward the man. "Make this the short version."

Pete saw his aunt squeeze Merle's arm.

"Dearly beloved. . ." The ceremony was over in five minutes, and the announcement was made. "You may kiss your bride."

Merle wrapped Aunt Ethel in his large embrace and kissed her soundly. "Finally, I'm a married man." He scooped his bride up and strode out of the church a happy man.

Aunt Ethel smiled and waved to Pete over Merle's shoulder.

Minister Hanson slapped him on the back. "When you asked if I had time for a wedding, I thought you were the one getting married."

"If the good Lord gives me the right words, and the girl is in the frame of mind to listen to a poor sap's tale and believe him, I might just ask her to be my wife."

"I'll be praying for you and this girl."

Pete walked to the police station and got permission to have his aeroplane back. He fueled up and felt the distinct lack of Fred's presence. *Lord, help me find Fred as soon as I land in Cashmere.*

After a safety check to make sure the officer who flew

Jenny hadn't hurt anything, Pete climbed aboard, started the engine, and pushed the throttle. Jenny zoomed across the field and off the ground, glad to be in the air again. He drew in a deep breath, thankful to be free and airborne once again.

fourteen

Lizzie blinked at the morning sun. It had to be nine or ten in the morning. She rose and made her repairs. Now, could she take off from this small, lumpy field? She checked the wind direction, then packed up.

Fred sat on his haunches and waved his paws at her to put him up in the aeroplane. "I'm coming. Just be patient." Fred stood on all fours and barked once with his tail wagging faster than a prop spun. She took him in one hand and used her other to pull herself up onto the wing. She settled in with Fred and drove Betty to the far corner, then got out and pushed the plane as far back near the pine trees as she could. She needed every foot she could get to have enough lift to climb over these tall pines.

Betty's engine purred once again. "This is it, Lord. Please get me over those trees." Lizzie took a deep breath, jammed the throttle forward, and bumped along the ground. *Please keep the wheels attached.* She picked up speed.

"Come on, get into the air, come on." Betty lifted off the ground and rose into the air but not steeply enough to miss the trees. Lizzie angled slightly off of the headwind she needed for lift to aim for an opening where a shorter tree stood. "Climb, Betty, climb."

She banked harder and caught the treetop as she skimmed by. She heaved a heavy sigh. She was clear. "Thank You, Lord!"

She scratched Fred's head. "We made it. We're safe now."

Fred put his paws on the side of the cockpit and hung his head out in the wind, his stubby tail wagging back and forth. Fred wasn't the only one glad to be back in the air.

Pete flew until his tank was dry and he had to glide down to the nearest field. He dumped his extra tank of gasoline in and took off as fast as he could. He wanted to make short work of the trip to Cashmere.

He landed in the same field and trekked for the Carter farmhouse. No one was home, and the Tin Lizzie was gone. He headed into town and went to Bill's Garage.

"Pete, it's good to see you," Finn said.

"I'm looking for Lizzie."

Finn's happy expression fell. "She's not with you?"

"No. Why would she be?"

"She took off yesterday, going to see you in Spokane. Take back your dog."

Fred? He was safe then. "Did she take the train?"

"No. She *took off*." Finn pointed his hand into the air like an aeroplane.

"She didn't fly?"

Finn nodded.

His gut clenched. "In what? Not her Bleriot?"

Finn nodded again.

"But it wasn't even finished."

"She finished it. I told her it was a fool's idea to fly it. But she was determined."

"She's only flown twice. How could she think she was capable of making the trip all the way to Spokane?" He raced out to the building Lizzie's Bleriot had been in to see for himself. Empty.

He ran back. Bill stood next to Finn. "I need gasoline. My tank is dry and so is my extra."

Bill filled an extra tank he had on hand and drove Pete out to his aeroplane, then made another trip with both his and Pete's extra tank. Jenny's tank was soon full, and so was the spare.

Finn put a hand on his shoulder. "You should have told her you were married."

Pete scowled. "I'm not married."

"But that woman?"

"Is not my wife. She lied."

Finn smiled. "I'm glad to hear that."

"I need to go."

"You think Lizzie made it okay?"

The trip shouldn't have taken her two days. Why hadn't he seen her along the way? Because he didn't know to look for her. He pictured Lizzie flying the way she drove—careless. "I don't know if her aeroplane was ready to fly. What route did she take?"

"I don't know." Finn said. "She's my flesh and blood. You find her and bring her back."

"She said something about following the train tracks," Bill noted.

It wasn't the most direct route, but it would get her there. If she stuck close to the line and landed someplace, he'd find her. And if she crashed. . .he'd find that, too.

❧

After one stop for more gasoline, and a lot of flying, Lizzie looked at the large city below. This must be Spokane. Pete had said there was a field that was the cat's meow on the north end of town near where he'd lived with his aunt.

She swung north and flew a back-and-forth pattern until she found a field that she thought could be the one Pete had spoken of and circled around to land. The ground was smooth and afforded her the space to turn her craft around at the end. She climbed down, then reached her arms up. "Come on, Fred."

Fred stood behind the pilot cockpit on the fuselage, did a little dance, then jumped into her arms. She scratched him. "Good boy."

She walked to the edge of the field and looked at the options of directions on the different streets. Which way should she go? She put her face right up to Fred's. He licked her over and over. She held him away from herself. "You know where Pete is, don't you? Find Pete for me." She set Fred down, and he looked up at her. "Home, Fred. Go home."

Fred wagged his tail, then took off running as fast as he could.

Back the way they'd come. She caught up to him at Betty. Fred stood wagging his tail looking from her to the aeroplane, back and forth.

She picked him up. "This isn't home." She ruffled his furry head. "Maybe this is home to you."

She walked back into town and started going up and down the near streets, hoping to run across Pete. How else was she going to find him? She saw a man on his porch and stopped. "Do you know where Pete Garfield lives?"

The older man puffed on his pipe. "Pete? Do you mean Lieutenant Garfield, our local war hero?"

"He's the one."

"Yes, he flew for the good guys in the Great War."

"I know."

The man pointed his pipe. "He has a dog just like yours."

"This is his dog. I'm trying to find him, so I can return him." And to say good-bye. "Do you know where he lives?"

"He always lived with his aunt. She's a strange one. Don't know how the boy turned out as good as he did."

Couldn't this man answer a simple question? "Where does she live?"

He pointed with his pipe again. "Down yonder a few blocks."

Yonder? "Do you know the street?"

"Nope." He popped the pipe back into his mouth.

Yonder. At least she had a direction. She set Fred down, took hold of the rope attached to his coat, and started off yonder. After a few blocks, she stopped and stared at a woman and little girl walking up the street in her direction. The little girl yelled, "Doggy," and ran ahead of her pregnant mother.

"Ruth, don't. Come back."

Ruth hugged Fred.

Lizzie recognized the woman as the one coming out of the jail. She must be Agatha. Pete's wife and child. The air froze in her lungs. She was prepared to see Pete but not his family.

Fred licked Ruth's face, and the girl giggled. Agatha grabbed her daughter's hand and pulled her away. "Stop that, Ruth."

Fred barked at Agatha, and she pulled back, narrowing her eyes at the dog. "Please tell me that's not Fred."

All Lizzie could do was nod.

Agatha's face twisted into a congenial smile, and she held out her hand. "You must be that Lizzie girl David told me about."

Who was David, and how would he know about her?

"This is my parents' house. Won't you come in for tea?"

❧

Pete hadn't found Lizzie's aeroplane anywhere along the train tracks, and Spokane was just ahead. He circled town, looking for the places he knew an aeroplane could land. His tank had to be nearly empty. He headed north to his regular landing field, the one he'd bought with his military pay.

He came around over a clump of trees. There sat Lizzie's Bleriot. She'd made it. All the way. *Thank You, Lord.*

He set down and drove Jenny over, parking directly in front of Lizzie's aeroplane. She didn't appear to be here, and he didn't want her taking off before he found her. Her aeroplane looked fine. He bent down and pulled a pine branch from her wheel riggings. He wasn't sure he wanted to know.

A black Tin Lizzie motored across the field, and David got

out. "I saw you flying overhead back and forth. I didn't expect you back so soon."

Pete swung out of the cockpit and leapt to the ground. "She's here."

David glanced at the other aeroplane. "Is that hers?"

Pete nodded.

"She's some doll."

Pete smiled. "That she is. Where do you think she'd go?"

"Why would I know? You stay here. She'll have to come back here eventually. I'll drive around."

"How will you recognize her?"

David shrugged. "She'll look out of place."

"I've parked so she can't leave. Drop me at the edge of town, and I'll walk the near streets."

David drove him to the first street.

"I'll take this street and stay south and head west. You stay to the north side and head east. We'll meet back at the aeroplanes at dusk." Which wasn't more than a couple of hours from now. "She has Fred with her."

David nodded and drove off.

❧

Lizzie sat alone in the ornate parlor, one knee bouncing violently. She slapped one hand over the other on it to stop the jitters. Fred raised his head from where he lay on the couch beside her. No one would notice if she slipped out the door.

But Agatha swept into the room like a floating angel. "She's down for her nap." Agatha and a servant had gone upstairs to the nursery.

Lizzie could hear the child crying. What it must be like to have servants and a house big enough to have a nursery.

Agatha sat in one of the chairs opposite her and widened her eyes. "The dog's not to be on the settee." She rose with her arms out as though she was going to take Fred.

Fred growled.

"Fine. He can stay since we have company." Agatha sat back down.

A different servant entered with a silver tray and set it on the coffee table. Lizzie took the cold glass of lemonade the woman offered. She handed a second glass to Agatha.

"Mrs. Porter, you've made us fresh lemonade." Agatha took the glass. "How thoughtful of you."

Mrs. Porter gave Agatha a quick look, nodded, and left the room, never saying a word.

"Pete flew all the way down to California last week to get these lemons for me. He's so thoughtful, always thinking of me."

Lizzie took a nervous sip of her drink. Lizzie had thought Pete was in jail. He'd said so in his letter. Just one more lie. "It's very good."

Agatha took a dainty sip and cradled her glass in her lap. "Pete is always doing the sweetest things for me. I think he feels guilty about being away so much. He loves being in the air. I'd never take that away from him. I think he would shrivel up and die if he couldn't fly." She gave a little twitter of a giggle.

Lizzie gave a nervous laugh in response. Pete did seem to be at home up in the sky.

Agatha laid a delicate hand on her chest. "It does scare me so when he does those stunts." She lowered her hand to her swollen belly. "I do so want my children to grow up with their father. He's such a good daddy."

Lizzie put her glass to her lips and drank half the liquid in two large gulps. She didn't know what to say. Did she tell this sweet woman that her husband had kissed Lizzie, that he wasn't everything she thought he was? Could she shatter this poor woman's illusion? Her knee started bouncing again.

Agatha went on to tell her how she and Pete had fallen in love and married before he'd gone off to war. She'd been pregnant and had little Ruth while her daddy was fighting the evil Germans.

How could Pete gypsy around when he had such a sweet, trusting wife and cute little daughter? How could he have told Lizzie that he loved her when he had a home here? He deserved to have his little world torn apart like he'd torn her heart apart. But could she hurt this angel sitting across from her? Her lungs tightened, and air refused to move in or out of them. "I should be going." Lizzie stood, and Fred jumped from the couch.

Agatha stood as well. "I'll see you to the door." At the door, Agatha picked up Fred. Fred wiggled in her arms as he growled.

Lizzie stepped out onto the porch. "It was nice meeting you."

"The pleasure was all mine. Do come back. I so enjoyed your visit."

There was no way Lizzie would be able to return, but she nodded anyway and turned to leave. She headed down the street with tears building in her eyes. Then she heard barking. Fred was at her side, so she picked him up.

Agatha flowed out to meet her. "I'm sorry about that." She took the dog even though it growled at her. "It's Pete's dog." Agatha flounced back into the house.

An automobile motored up and slid to a stop. "Lizzie?"

She stared at the brown-haired man. How did he know her name?

He jumped out and came around his Ford.

She backed away from him. "Do I know you?"

He took off his hat and bowed. "David Powers. I'm a friend of Pete's."

She wiped a tear off of each cheek. "Tell Pete good-bye for me." She didn't need to see him face-to-face anymore. "I left Fred with his wife." She pointed back toward the house.

"Wife? You mean Agatha? Poor dog. Let's go get him, as

well as the truth." He took her arm and led her back to the house.

She stopped at the bottom step. "I don't want to go."

"Agatha's not Pete's wife."

"But she told me how they fell in love and everything."

"Agatha didn't quite tell you the truth. And I think she should be the one to tell you that herself." He guided her up the steps and used the knocker.

Agatha opened the door with a smile, but it quickly faded. "David."

He stepped inside, pulling Lizzie with him.

"I'm really not up for company at the moment," Agatha stammered.

"Agatha, you look tired. Do have a seat." He helped the pregnant woman to a chair, then offered the couch to Lizzie, who sat. Fred jumped up next to her.

"Now, Agatha, this young lady is under the impression that you're married to Pete Garfield." He spoke softly as though to an errant child. "I'm quite surprised by this news as I'm your fiancé!"

Agatha's sweet demeanor turned hard and mean. "Very well. I'm not married to Pete."

Pete wasn't married. Lizzie's heart leapt for joy at the news. "And?"

"What? I told her the truth."

"Your children? Who's the father?"

"I'm not admitting that."

"Is Pete the father?"

She narrowed a wicked gaze at David. "No. Are you happy?"

"Not really." He stood and offered a hand to Lizzie. "Shall we go now?"

Lizzie stood, stunned. Pete not only wasn't married, but he wasn't the father of this cruel woman's children.

David picked up Fred. "We're taking Fred."

"Good. I can't stand that motley beast." Agatha glared at Lizzie. "Pete can have the little tramp. See if I care."

David shook his head at Agatha. "I don't know what I ever saw in you. I'm not going to marry you after all." He turned and walked out the door with Lizzie.

When they were halfway to David's Ford, Agatha screamed from the porch, "David, you can't do this to me."

David turned and gave her a bow. "Give my regards to my brother when you tell his wife he has an illegitimate child and another on the way." He held open the door for Lizzie.

She stared ahead as David motored down the street. "Pete really isn't married?"

"Nope."

"He doesn't have a wife, and Ruth's not his daughter?"

"Nope. He's out looking for you right now. It's nearly dusk. He'll be heading back to the aeroplanes soon. We'll meet him there."

Lizzie couldn't believe it. Those weren't Pete's pregnant wife and child. She'd come to say good-bye, but now she didn't have to. She threw her hands into the air. "He's not married!"

૨૪

It was too dark to see anything anymore. Pete finally resigned himself to not finding Lizzie tonight and pointed his feet toward the field. When he broke into the opening, he could see the distant glow of a fire. That would be David. As he strode closer, he could hear voices. A man and a woman.

Had David found Lizzie? His stomach did a double loop and a roll.

He stopped a few feet away around the end of the tail of his aeroplane in the shadows and out of sight. *Please let her understand.*

He wasn't sure how to announce himself so he gave a short whistle out of the side of his mouth. Fred came running and jumped up into his arms. The dog thoroughly licked his face.

Pete stepped around the end of the aeroplane and saw a figure charging at him. He set Fred down so the dog wouldn't get hurt. Was she going to hit him or something? Instead, she threw her arms around his neck, nearly knocking him off his feet.

"Pete!"

He held her and kissed her while he had the chance, then said, "Lizzie, I'm so sorry for all this trouble. I can explain."

"No need. I already know everything. She's not your wife, and you're not the father of her children."

"Then you forgive me?"

"For what? You didn't do anything."

He held her close again and nestled his face into her hair. "I missed you."

"I missed you, too."

"I never want to lose you again. Marry me, Lizzie."

She pushed him away. "Pete Garfield, don't toy with me."

Pete clasped her hands and got down on his knees. "I'm not. I love you and want more than anything for you to be my wife." He didn't want to risk losing her again.

Fred sat up on his haunches and waved his paws.

"See, even Fred's begging."

fifteen

Lizzie stared down at Pete on his knees. Was he serious? Or was this a flight of fancy? She'd come with the intent of saying good-bye. This was such a turnabout. Everything was happening so fast. How did she feel? Were her own feelings deep enough and strong enough to support a marriage?

"I'm just not sure." She was worried that he would be put off by her doubt.

Pete jumped to his feet, held her hands together, and kissed each one. "I'll prove myself worthy of your love. No matter how long it takes."

She was glad her uncertainty hadn't dampened his enthusiasm. She wanted to say yes but should wait until her jumble of emotions settled down.

David cleared his throat, and they both turned to him. "It's getting real cold out here. Can I interest either of you in a lift?"

"Lizzie, this is my best friend—wait, you two have already met." He put his hand on David's shoulder. "You mind taking us to my aunt's?"

"The fire's already put out, and Fred's in the Tin Lizzie. I just need you two to hop in."

"Let me grab my bag." Lizzie climbed up and retrieved it, and Pete threw it in the front passenger seat, then offered her the backseat and climbed in next to her. Fred and David occupied the front.

Pete turned to her. "I can't believe you got that thing to fly."

She gasped. "You doubted my abilities? I followed the instructions."

"I still can't believe you flew all the way here. You're amazing, simply amazing." Pete patted David's shoulder. "You see why I love her. She isn't afraid of anything."

She basked in Pete's praise. She wanted to snuggle in his arms and never come out but sat properly in her seat.

Pete leaned close to her ear and whispered, "I like your hair."

She touched the shorter style. She'd hoped he would. After she'd whacked it off, she'd gone the following day to a beauty salon to have it evened up.

David pulled up to an apartment building, and Pete helped her out and took her bag. "David, you're coming in, aren't you?"

"I don't want to impose."

"Nonsense. Aunt Ethel will be glad to see you."

The four went inside and up to the top floor. A woman with bleached blond hair greeted them. "Pete, you're back so soon. David, it's good to have you back. And this must be Lizzie." The woman grabbed her and nearly squeezed the breath out of her.

"Lizzie, this is my aunt Ethel, and this is Uncle Merle." Pete pointed to a distinguished-looking man standing behind Aunt Ethel.

"Pleased to meet you."

"Come in and sit down." Aunt Ethel waved them all into the living room.

David held up a hand. "I can't stay. It's getting late. I just wanted to pop in and say hello."

Pete turned to David. "Can you give Lizzie a ride to the O'Toole Hotel?"

"I'm not staying at a hotel. I'm sleeping under my aeroplane."

Pete shook his head. "It's too cold for that."

"But—"

"You covered it. It will be safe from deer. I promise. Stay at the hotel."

"Nonsense," Aunt Ethel piped up. "You'll stay in Pete's room."

"Aunt Ethel! She can't stay in my room."

Lizzie could tell that Pete was flabbergasted at his aunt's proposal. She was taken aback, as well.

Aunt Ethel twisted her hands onto her hips. "Well, you're not going to be in there."

Pete stared at his aunt. "Where am I going to be?"

"I don't know. Somewhere else." Aunt Ethel waved a hand toward him. "You can't stay here. You two aren't married yet."

"Aunt Ethel, don't."

"Don't what? You are going to marry her? She flew all this way."

Lizzie's heart did a little dance at the mention of marriage to Pete again. She wanted to marry him; she just wasn't sure if he was really serious.

Pete leaned closer to his aunt. "We haven't really discussed marriage."

Lizzie suspected he was trying to spare her feelings of embarrassment.

"Well, get a move on. You don't want someone else to steal her away from you." Aunt Ethel patted Pete on the arm. "Now you go. Stay at David's."

David piped up then. "That's kind of a long story, but I don't think I'll be welcome at home. My brother's a bit sore at me, and I don't really want to stay there right now."

"I'll stay at a hotel, and Pete and David can stay here." Lizzie didn't want to put anyone out.

"I won't hear of it." Aunt Ethel turned to Pete. "You two go. I want to get to know Lizzie."

Merle held out a key. "You boys can stay at my house."

"Hot dog." David snatched the key. "I'll meet you down at the Tin Lizzie."

Pete took Lizzie's hand and led her to the door. "Please

don't be put off by Aunt Ethel. She's definitely a modern woman with very progressive ideals."

"She seems very nice and agreeable. I like your aunt."

"Just don't let her scare you off. I need a chance to prove myself to you."

Lizzie smiled at him. "I don't think you have anything to worry about."

"She can come on a little strong."

"And you don't?"

He gave her a smart-alecky face. "But you love me. Remember, you said that."

She remembered, but she wasn't going to tell him. She just gave him an impish smile to keep him wondering.

He kissed her hand, then held it to his chest. "I'll see you tomorrow."

She was looking forward to it.

❧

After Lizzie dressed the following morning, she sat at the kitchen table with a cup of hot coffee, waiting for Pete to show up. Pete's aunt walked in robed in a feathery housecoat that made her look as though she was floating.

"Good morning, Mrs. . . . I'm sorry. I forgot your last name." Lizzie stood and poured the older woman a cup of coffee.

"Call me Aunt Ethel." Aunt Ethel smoothed the feathers away from her face and accepted the cup. "You'll be part of the family soon."

Lizzie could feel her cheeks warm. "I don't know about that."

Aunt Ethel pinched her eyebrows together. "He has proposed, hasn't he?"

He had, but she didn't think that really counted.

"He did say you hadn't talked about it, but I just thought that was his polite way of telling me to shut my mouth."

Aunt Ethel patted her hand. "Don't you fret none over it. I'll speak to Pete about marrying you."

"Oh no, please don't." She didn't want Pete proposing because someone was pressuring him to do so. She wanted it to come from his heart.

"Aunt Ethel will take care of everything." The older woman took a sip of her coffee.

Lizzie wanted to sink into the chair and disappear. Better yet, run outside and catch Pete before he could come inside and have his aunt coerce him. She startled at the knock on the door, nearly spilling her coffee.

Aunt Ethel opened the door, and David walked in.

Alone.

Lizzie jumped to her feet. "Where's Pete?" If he was right behind David, she wanted to intercept him before his aunt could get to him.

"I don't exactly know. He said he had something he had to do. He told me to tell you not to worry and he'd see you this afternoon."

Well, that was disappointing. She'd wanted to see him early but was glad Aunt Ethel wouldn't be able to talk to him yet. Lizzie needed to figure out how to tell Pete not to listen to his aunt when she told him to marry her without giving him the impression she didn't want to marry him. She sighed. An impossible task.

Lord, if Pete decides to propose, let it be from his heart and let me know somehow that his proposal is because he wants to marry me and not because he feels obligated.

❧

Pete took a deep breath, then opened the door to the Cashmere Post Office.

"What do you want?" Mr. Carter was obviously not happy to see him. But then, Mr. Carter didn't know the truth.

"I was hoping to talk to you."

"Where's Elizabeth?"

He furrowed his brow. "Who? Oh, you mean Lizzie."

"Her name is Elizabeth."

Pete figured it was best if he didn't push that one. "Elizabeth's in Spokane."

A sad expression crossed the older man's face. "Is she coming back?"

"As far as I know. Can I take you to lunch?"

"I don't have anything to say to you." He gimped away, then turned back. "Wait. There is one thing. I'm sorry I had the whiskey put in your aeroplane, but I'm not sorry Elizabeth found out about your wife."

"Mr. Carter, I don't have a wife." But he wanted one. This was not the time to tell Mr. Carter that. "Or any children. That was a lie. . . ." He debated whether or not to say his next thought, but it came out anyway. "Just like the bootleg, and I'd like the opportunity to clear it all up in your mind."

Mr. Carter eyed him with suspicion. "Does Elizabeth know about your wife?"

Pete gritted his teeth. "Agatha's not my wife." He took a slow breath. It wouldn't help him any to let his anger loose. He relaxed his jaw. "Please have lunch with me, and I'll explain everything. You at least owe me that." He hoped to play on the man's guilty conscience.

Mr. Carter reluctantly agreed, so Pete took him to a diner down the street. Pete told Mr. Carter the whole long, involved story.

"A week ago I wouldn't have believed you. No, I wouldn't have even sat down to listen to you." The older man rose, shaking his head. "People just aren't who I thought they were." He started to leave, then turned back. "My grandfather lied about my father and my mother. My wife ran away with another man. I told Elizabeth and Ivan she went to see her ailing sister back East. The automobile she was in ran off the road. She was killed. Learning the truth hurts, but not as much as the lies."

"Wait. I wanted to ask you something."

"What is it?"

His gut knotted. "I want your permission. . .to marry Li—Elizabeth."

"I'd say no, but I think she'll do what she wants anyway."

But he didn't say yes. "Does that mean I have your permission to ask her?"

"If I say no, will you go away?"

He shook his head. "I'll hang around until I grow on you."

Mr. Carter frowned. "Are you going to take her away from here?"

"Cashmere's kind of grown on me. It's a sweet little town. I figure I can open a flying school."

"You'll never make enough to feed yourself. How are you going to feed a family?"

"Oh, there are plenty of people who want to learn to fly. I could also fly the mail, provide service from Wenatchee to Spokane and to Seattle."

Mr. Carter narrowed his eyes. "You've thought this all out, haven't you?"

"Yes, sir."

"I suppose if Elizabeth's going to marry someone someday, it might as well be you." Mr. Carter slumped his shoulders in defeat.

Pete beamed a smile. Now all he had to do was convince Lizzie he was the right fella, too.

"I'll bring Elizabeth back tomorrow."

Mr. Carter raised his eyebrows.

"There won't be enough daylight to fly back today, but I want you to know that she's staying at my aunt's, and I'm staying elsewhere."

"So you forgive me for the bootleg?"

He put a hand on the old man's shoulder. "Life's too short to hold grudges."

≈

Lizzie'd had a great day with Aunt Ethel. It was nearing supper, and the setting sun cast an orange glow on the western clouds. Where was Pete? She'd gone out to the field where her Bleriot and Pete's Jenny had been parked together. Hers stood alone draped in canvas. He couldn't fly in the dark. If he didn't return soon, he'd be stuck wherever he was. Then she had a terrifying thought. *Lord, please let Pete be all right. Don't let him have crashed someplace.*

Lizzie wadded the cloth she was supposed to be wiping the kitchen table with, twisting it around and around her fingers.

"You're going to lose a finger if you pull that any tighter."

She looked up at Aunt Ethel and tossed the rag onto the counter. "Do you think Pete's all right? You don't think he's crashed or anything?"

"He survived the Great War, didn't he?"

Maybe that would be a small comfort if he'd actually fought in the war. Even if he had, that wouldn't stop an accident from taking his life now.

A key rattled in the lock of the front door. Lizzie held her breath until Merle stepped inside. She quickly said hello to him then hurried to Pete's room and closed the door. Tears burned the back of her eyes. Pete had to be all right. But what if. . . ? She couldn't think about that. She took a deep breath to calm herself. Pete was fine. She had to believe that. She smoothed her dress and went back out.

Pete stood in the kitchen talking with Aunt Ethel and Merle. She just stared at him, drinking in the sight of his living self. He turned and gifted her with his charming smile. "Lizzie." He came over and slipped his arm around her waist. "Isn't she beautiful?" he said to his aunt and uncle.

Merle hugged Aunt Ethel and picked her up. "Not as pretty as my Ethel."

She had to smile at the obvious love. She'd not seen that between her parents before her mom had left.

Aunt Ethel giggled. "Put me down. You're embarrassing the kids."

Merle obeyed. "Sorry."

"We'll be leaving first thing tomorrow," Pete said.

"I was hoping it wouldn't come so soon. Where are you two off to?" Aunt Ethel asked.

"I'm taking Lizzie back home. I'll fly her out in my aeroplane, stay the weekend, ride the train back, and get her aeroplane." He spoke matter-of-factly.

Lizzie planted her fists on her hips. He hadn't even consulted her. "I can fly my own aeroplane back."

"I can't let you do that. It's too risky."

She could tell he was trying to protect her, but it made her mad. She'd flown out here; she could fly back. And she would. "Why would it be more risky for me to fly my craft that I know better than anyone, than you, who have never flown her?" She wanted to make sure he understood that she was more than qualified to fly it herself.

"You've only flown three times. You don't have the experience to handle an emergency."

She could brag about how she handled her little emergency but thought he might turn it against her as a reason she shouldn't fly. "If I never fly, how can I get experience?"

Pete tried to start several times but failed to make a sentence or even a complete word.

"I'll bet you got your experience by flying." She didn't like the double standard.

Pete just stared at her.

She didn't like Pete telling her what she could and couldn't do without discussing it with her and turned back to Aunt

Ethel and Merle, who were both smiling. "I'll be leaving tomorrow. Flying my own aeroplane back."

Pete sputtered beside her.

Aunt Ethel's smile broadened. "I like you, Lizzie Carter."

⋧

Lizzie circled Johnson's field. Pete motioned for her to land first. She came around to line up with the field and headed down. She eased Betty down and made her smoothest landing yet. She removed her goggles and shaded her eyes in the late afternoon sun to watch Pete bring in Jenny. A smooth, perfect landing. She'd make those one day.

It had been a good thing they had flown side by side. Pete's engine had gone out on him, and she'd been able to land in the same field. He'd flown Betty to a nearby town and gotten what he needed to fix Jenny. Pete had used the experience as a lesson, asking Lizzie what she would have done.

Pete swiped off his helmet as he jumped down and ruffled his hair. Her breath caught. He was as magnificent as the first day he'd flown into her life.

"Let's cover our aeroplanes, and I'll walk you home."

They covered Betty first, then Jenny. As she tied the last rope around Jenny's tail, Lizzie did so as slowly as possible.

"You ready?"

She looped one end of the rope around the other one last time and pulled. "I don't want to go."

He turned her to face him. "Why?"

"I can't even look at him after what he did. I don't know if I can forgive him."

"But you have to."

"Why?"

"None of us deserves to be forgiven, but God does it anyway. When you refuse to forgive someone, you hurt yourself more than you do the person you are trying to punish." He reached down and plucked a tuft of dry grass, then folded it into her hand. "Hold on to that."

She didn't know why he wanted her to, but she squeezed her hand.

"That grass is dead. Useless. As long as you hold onto it, your hand is also useless." He peeled her fingers back one at a time. "You can't knit. . .or cook. . .or drive. . .or fly as long as you hold on to that grass."

He'd peeled back all but one of her fingers. "When you hold on to others' transgressions against you, you are useless. Let it go, Lizzie. Let go."

Let go? Was he telling her to let go of more than the grass and the hurt, but him as well? He smiled at her. She opened her last finger on her own, and the breeze snatched the grass away. She knew that forgiveness wasn't quite so easy, but she also knew she had to forgive her father because she didn't want to be useless. She didn't want to be in bondage because she couldn't forgive.

"Now your hand is useful." He took her hand and gave it a squeeze. "Let's go before it gets dark."

She stood her ground, and Pete gave her a confused look. "If you don't mind, I'd like to walk alone and think about what you said before I face Daddy."

He nodded, then lifted her hand and kissed the back of it. "I'll see you tomorrow."

"Really?"

"I'll be right here."

She walked away and looked back several times. Pete remained rooted in place.

She reached the driveway of her home just as Ivan drove the Ford up to the house and stopped it with a jerk. She watched Daddy struggle out of the automobile and up the steps. The pain of Daddy's betrayal rippled through her. How could Daddy have hurt her like this?

She saw Daddy and Ivan move past the window inside.

Lord, give me the courage to go inside and forgive. She saw a stoop-shouldered figure move across the kitchen window. Was that Grandpa? Her feet propelled her forward, up the steps, and through the front door.

Grandpa was setting a plate of biscuits on the table next to the cast-iron pot that smelled of beans. Daddy sat at his usual place at the head of the table, and Ivan in his seat next to him. All three stared at her; then Daddy stood. "I didn't think you were coming back."

"I said I'd come back."

Daddy walked around the table and stood a few feet in front of her. "I was beginning to think I wouldn't get this chance, so I'm taking it. The good Lord has seen fit to wrestle with me these few days you've been gone and has shown me the error of my ways. What I did to you was uncalled for. I understand if you don't have forgiveness in your heart for me right now. But I'm begging you for your forgiveness."

She could feel her short nails digging into her palms. When had she fisted her hands? She made a conscious effort to unfurl her fingers. . .and let go. "I forgive you." Love and peace washed over her. She stepped forward as her arms swung around him. "I love you, Daddy."

sixteen

Lizzie ran and ran until she came to the edge of the Johnsons' field and wrapped her arms around a small tree trunk to keep herself up as she struggled for air. Pete's Jenny sat in the middle of the field. He held the rapt attention of his audience of young ladies.

She had to tell him.

She tried to call out to him but could only gasp. She would give herself a moment to catch her breath.

Pete kissed each of the seven girls, then climbed aboard his aeroplane.

No!

She pushed away from the tree, still gasping, and ran as fast as she could after Pete's aeroplane. "Pete! Pete!"

He went faster and faster, but surprisingly, she was able to keep up. She called and called and reached for the yellow tail. Her fingers grazed the fabric as the craft broke free of the ground and slipped from her grasp.

"Pete!"

She had to tell him.

The Jenny rose up into the air and circled the field. Pete waved to the crowd of girls, then blew them a kiss.

Lizzie jumped and waved her arms over her head. "Pete!"

Pete flew low over her, smiled, and gave her a final salute good-bye before flying off into the clouds.

"Pete! Come back!" She would never see him again. She dropped to her knees and sobbed into her hands. She never got to tell him.

"Lizzie. Lizzie?"

She opened her eyes and sucked in a gulp of air at Ivan standing over her bed.

"You were hollering in your sleep." Ivan raked a hand through his disheveled brown hair. "I got an examination today."

She sat up and rubbed her face. "I'm sorry."

Ivan shuffled out.

Lizzie lay back down and stared toward the ceiling. A backlash of emotion trickled from her eyes. What had she wanted to tell Pete?

As dawn began to gray the horizon outside her window, she dressed and began her morning chores. She completed them all before taking Daddy to the post office, then she hurried to Johnson's field. She had to see Pete.

❧

After more than a month since they'd returned from Spokane, Pete was still in the Cashmere area. He spent a lot of time in Wenatchee and was gone for days at a time. He always returned, but she knew that one day he might fly away for good. *He's a gypsy. Gypsies always leave.* Pete hadn't mentioned marriage again since Spokane. Did he even think about it? She thought about it daily and wished she'd said yes when he'd asked. Would he ever ask again?

The yellow Jenny was motoring across the field. She raced after it, nearly catching up, but it lifted off the ground and soared over the trees. She stopped her Model T and got out, waving her arms, but Pete did not circle back around to see her.

Then, just like in her dream, she dropped to her knees and cried, covering her face with her hands. Would she ever see him again? Had he decided to leave for good? She didn't get to tell him. She still didn't know what she'd wanted to tell him in her dream, but she knew what she wanted to tell him now.

She loved him and hadn't told him so since that day he was

arrested in this very field. The words had flown from her lips then, though not grounded in any forethought. She hadn't known if she loved him then or not. The words had just been ripped from her. She had never regretted saying them, nor had she intended to say them again until she was sure.

She was sure now.

Was it too late?

Or was it always too late?

આ

Pete sat in the growing darkness on Lizzie's porch. He blew into his cold hands. Soon he saw headlights from Lizzie's Tin Lizzie approach. He stood when the Model T came to a stop. Ivan, Mr. Carter, and Finn all greeted him. Finn had moved in with his family, and everyone seemed to be happy with the arrangement. Pete, for one, was glad to see that Finn had a permanent place to live in the waning years of his life.

Finn and Mr. Carter had worked out their differences and forgiven each other. They'd even said that they'd both forgiven Great-grandpa Carter. Lizzie had forgiven her dad. And even the sheriff had apologized for his part in it all. Pete had been tempted to hold a grudge against the man but felt so much better when he forgave the man and shook his hand in friendship.

Lizzie stood next to the Ford with her arms folded. She looked upset. It couldn't be at him. He hadn't been around all day, and the last time he'd seen her, he'd left her smiling. Maybe he'd misread her, and she wasn't really upset.

"Hey, Lizzie." He strode toward her.

She didn't respond.

"Is something wrong?"

"You just flew away this morning without looking back."

He pulled his eyebrows together. "Were you at the field?"

She nodded.

"I didn't see you. If I had, I would have stopped or come

back." He moved forward with his arms out to hold her.

She stepped back, then walked around the rear of the Ford.

He caught up with her at the front corner and held her by the upper arms. "What's wrong?"

"Why don't you just leave? You're going to anyway." She sniffled, and a lone tear trickled down her cheek.

"What are you talking about?"

"You're always gone, sometimes for days. Eventually, you'll fly away and never return. The sooner you do that, the better." Another tear fell.

Pete brushed away the two tears with his thumbs. "Lizzie, I'm not planning on leaving. I like it here. It's comfortable. Kind of like a broken-in flying helmet. It helps you fly off and brings you back home again. This is where I want to be."

"For how long? You'll grow restless and want to leave eventually."

He'd put off proposing to her again until he had everything in place so he'd be sure she'd have the confidence in him to say yes. He took her hands. "Let me show you what I've been doing. Meet me at the field tomorrow morning." He wanted to soothe all her fears.

Her bottom lip quivered, but she said, "Okay."

He gave her a gentle kiss on the lips.

"Do you want to come in for supper?" she asked. "It won't be ready for a while yet."

"I was hoping you'd ask." He took her by the hand and led her inside. Tomorrow she would see just how committed he was to sticking around.

❧

The next day, Lizzie drove across the field toward Pete's Jenny parked next to hers, which was draped in canvas to keep the animals away. Mr. Johnson had been very generous to let them use his land. Next to the aeroplanes, Pete had pitched a tent for himself. He slept in it most nights, but on the really cold, late-October nights, he stayed at Bill's. He was staying at Bill's more and more.

She parked and got out.

Pete greeted her with a hug and a kiss. "I just need to adjust the wires on the left wing, and we'll be ready to go. Go ahead and climb aboard. Fred's already in the seat."

She did, putting Fred on her lap, and watched Pete work. She remembered what Pete had told her over two months ago about her not being as modern as she thought she was. He was right. If she was truly a modern girl, she'd propose to him. She was not that bold.

Pete hadn't mentioned marriage, and he hadn't proposed again. But between his going off for days and her working at Liberty Orchard making candy all day now that the season was in full swing, she didn't get to spend as much time with him as she wanted to. And the time they did spend was usually around her family's table. Not much time alone.

Grandpa had jumped in with helping and even did some of the cooking. It was nice to come home to supper, even if it was only beans and biscuits. Daddy even talked about moving into town.

Lizzie did not want to get her hopes up about Pete's surprise. She'd thought a lot about Pete yesterday and realized he was not the kind of fellow who settled down and took a wife. He was a gypsy and needed to move around. Every day was one day closer to the time he would leave.

Pete gave her a blanket to keep warm and gifted her with a smile.

How many more of those would she get?

He flew over the trees and to Wenatchee ten miles away, landing on a field that looked like it was designed for aeroplanes to land on its smooth terrain.

Pete pulled up by one of the buildings and stopped, then helped her down.

"What is this place? I didn't know Wenatchee had a landing field."

Pete smiled. "It does now." He waved his hand toward the top of the high hangar building. GARFIELD-SPENCER FLYING SCHOOL.

"Is that you?" She pointed toward the sign.

Pete hooked his thumbs in the waist of his pants. "Sure is. I met this guy Spencer at the hardware store. We got to talking, and I found out he was a pilot, too. We pooled what we had and made a down payment on this land. I've been working with Spencer to smooth the runway."

"This is what you've been doing? Why didn't you tell me?"

"I wanted it to be a surprise. Come inside and meet Spencer, and I'll show you around." He took her inside and introduced her to a beanpole of a man who had to be over six foot six inches with wiry black hair.

Spencer shook her hand. "Pleased to finally meet you. And welcome to the team."

She looked from Spencer to Pete.

Pete leaned toward Spencer. "I haven't told her yet."

"Told me what?"

"We want you to work here with us." Pete handed her a set of leather flying togs. "These are for you."

She should be excited but found herself disappointed. This was no marriage proposal or a ring, only a job offer. Her heart sank. "Can I think about it?"

"Of course," Pete said to her, then leaned toward Spencer. "She'll take it. She won't be able to stay away."

Would she? Taking this position would mean giving up her dream of ever getting married. Did Pete only think of her as a potential partner and not as a potential wife? Did he regret proposing on a whim?

Pete showed her around, then flew her back to Cashmere.

She was warmer in her leather flying gear than with the blanket.

"Wait here. Fred has something for you." Pete took Fred into his tent and returned a moment later with Fred limping at his side.

"He's hurt." She rushed over.

Pete knelt beside Fred, who raised the offending paw. He had something on it. She knelt to see what it was. Fred rose up on his haunches and waved his front paws at her. She took the one paw and saw that there was a diamond ring tied to it. She sucked in a breath.

Pete untied it. "Will you marry me?"

"Are you sure?" It's what she wanted, but not if he didn't really want to stay. "You would have to stay here and not fly all over the country."

"That's why I built a flying school, so I could stay." He raised her to her feet. "Look around." He turned her in a circle in the field. "Everything you see is mine. Or will be mine when I get it paid off."

"What? Since when? No, it's not."

"I bought it from Mr. Johnson three weeks ago." He led her by the hand to the corner of the field. A rock foundation had been started. "I'm building you a house. I told you I'd prove to you that I was serious. Tell me what else to do, and I'll do it."

Tears sprang to her eyes. He really did want to stay. "Yes, I'll marry you."

He slipped the ring onto her finger, then swooped her into his arms and kissed her.

"I love you, Pete."

He smiled. "I know."

"You do? How?"

"You told me once. I figured if you ever changed your mind, you'd tell me."

"And?"

"And what?"

"You're supposed to tell me you love me, too."

He caressed her face. "Don't you know how much I love you? I'd do just about anything for you."

"A girl likes to hear it."

"I love you, the future Mrs. Pete Garfield." He kissed her again.

"How soon can we get married?"

Pete waved a hand toward the unfinished foundation. "I don't have a house for you yet."

"I don't care."

"I do. You can help me plan it out."

"Can I help you build it, too?"

Pete shook his head. "You really are amazing. What other doll would want to help build a house?"

"One who wants to get married to the man she loves."

seventeen

Six months later

Two days before the wedding in Cashmere, Pete put the last of his tools into his toolbox that Lizzie had bought him. He surveyed the first floor of his and Lizzie's recently completed house. There was no furniture yet. That had been due to arrive yesterday but hadn't. Maybe sometime today. Everything would be set on their wedding day.

He'd had offers to fly some stunts, but he'd turned them down. He didn't want to widow his bride before they were even married. He'd waited a long time for a special doll like Lizzie; he wanted to spend at least fifty years growing old with her.

He stood in the empty room and waited for that choking feeling he'd been expecting every day since Lizzie agreed to marry him to overtake him. But it never came. He never once had doubts that putting down roots with her was going to be a struggle. The roots that had already grown had grown out of his love for Lizzie and had been a source of strength for him. He was more afraid of Lizzie changing her mind than of being tethered to the ground, but Lizzie seemed more excited than he to get married. She was finally going to be his wife and move in.

Gratitude overwhelmed him, and he dropped to his knees. *Lord, You have blessed me beyond measure. You took a poor orphan boy with nothing and gave him the world.*

A knock interrupted him, and he went to the door. Lizzie stood rosy-cheeked like a breath of fresh spring air on the porch. He took her hand and pulled her inside. "I finished the tiles in the kitchen. Come see." He pulled her to the other room. He'd found the pale blue and pink tiles she'd wanted and had set them in all the countertops. He hoped she liked it. When she didn't say anything, he turned to her.

She wasn't even looking at the kitchen; instead she studied him. "I love you."

He kissed her. "I love you, too. Do you like it?"

"It's perfect."

"None of the furniture is here yet. It should come today. I hope it's here before the wedding."

"Even if it's not, that's fine."

"I want your house to be perfect."

"This house has everything in it right now to be perfect."

He frowned. "It's empty."

"It has you. That's all I need."

"And all I need is you."

A holler came from outside. "Yoo-hoo!"

Lizzie smiled and bit her bottom lip. "I have a surprise for you." She pulled him by the hand out the front door. "You said it didn't matter that you didn't have much family to come to the wedding."

A crowd of strangers, about a dozen, stood smiling up at the two of them. In front were Aunt Ethel and Uncle Merle. Who were the other people? His gaze fixed on an older woman with black hair. Even well into her forties, she had an arresting beauty about her. Without prodding, his feet propelled him forward to the woman. He could never forget those loving violet eyes. "Miss Vivian."

"Hello, Peter."

He took her hand and kissed it. "You saved my life." When he was an orphan living on the streets of Port Townsend with four other orphans, Miss Vivian had brought them food so they wouldn't have to go hungry or steal. Then she had helped build an orphanage to give the unwanted children a home.

He turned to the man standing next to her. "Mr. Jackson."

"It's Conner." Conner shook his hand.

He met Ruby, Vivian and Conner's adopted daughter with flaming red hair and a clubfoot. Unable to have children of their own, they had adopted Ruby when she was eight and later had adopted three other children. She was a lovely young lady in her early twenties. They still lived in Port Townsend and ran the general store as well as helped with Carlyle Shipping and the orphanage.

He saw Abigail, who still ran the orphanage, standing next to her husband, Martin. He shook hands with Harry, Abigail's son with whom he'd played as a child. Harry now had five younger siblings.

Pete next shook hands with a strapping man he remembered. "George." George had been the oldest of the orphans, and by the way he held the woman beside him, Pete would say she was George's wife. She held a two-year-old girl on her hip.

"You remember Betsy?" George looked lovingly at the woman.

"You're Betsy?" She didn't look anything like the scrawny, sad girl who always kept her head down.

"Pipe down. That ain't polite." Betsy said in an all-too-familiar tone, then smiled. She was always trying to get him to watch what he said and to behave.

"I never would have recognized you."

She was a woman of simple beauty. "This is our son, Malcolm." A boy of ten stood next to George.

He shook the boy's hand. "It's good to meet you."

"Where are Samuel and Tommy?" he asked George.

"They joined a ship's crew when they were old enough." Sadness crossed George's face. "It went down more than ten years ago."

Then Pete came to the last in the crowd, a stooped-shouldered old lady. She held out her hand to him. "It's Maggie."

He took her hand. Maggie had been Miss Vivian's house-keeper. "You made the best fried chicken."

Maggie smiled and patted his hand. "I'm glad you liked it."

He stepped back and looked at the crowd. This was his family. Not by blood, but by choice.

Two days later

Lizzie's breath caught when she saw Pete smiling at her from the front of the packed church. She was finally going to be his wife. She'd feared over the months that he'd change his mind and realize he didn't want to stay put, even for her. But he seemed happy in Cashmere, and his flying school was thriving and growing. He and his partner, Spencer, had even signed a contract to fly the mail routes between Wenatchee and Spokane and Seattle. Fred sat at Pete's feet.

Daddy squeezed her hand. "I like the boy."

Tears welled. "Oh, Daddy, that means so much to me." Daddy had sold the small farm and moved into town with Ivan and Grandpa. The three were getting on well and had hired a woman to come cook and clean. Mrs. Altman had helped Lizzie with her wedding dress. Lizzie was glad not to have to worry over Daddy so much.

"I tried hard not to like him."

She knew the feeling. She'd tried not to like Pete either because she never expected him to stay, but there was something about him that wrapped around her heart.

She and Daddy stopped at the front, and Daddy gave her away. He kissed her on the cheek. "I love you, Elizabeth."

She would always be Elizabeth to Daddy, but he'd accepted that other people called her Lizzie. "I love you, too, Daddy." Daddy sat down next to Grandpa Finn and Ivan.

She took Pete's arm and finally was able to take her vows

and start her life as a married woman.

After Pastor Littleman pronounced them husband and wife and Pete had kissed her for the first time as his wife, everyone proceeded to the reception at her brand-new, yet empty, house. The furniture still had not arrived.

Pete's friend David stood next to the red-haired beauty named Ruby. She was one of the group of people Aunt Ethel had rounded up, all of whom were proud to call Pete family. David had garnered one of the two window seats for Ruby to get off her poor leg. The elderly Maggie held the other window seat.

Pete came up and hooked his arm around Lizzie's waist. "It's time for you to go up and change so we can take off."

"So soon?"

"We need the daylight."

"Where are you taking me?"

Pete put his index finger on her lips. "Shh. I can't tell you that. It's a surprise."

She rushed upstairs, anxious for them to be on their way, and returned with her one small bag that Pete had said she could take along. Everyone poured out of the house to send the couple off. Someone had tied red fabric strips to Jenny's wing wires, and a banner lay on the ground behind her. Lizzie and Pete went over to it. *Just Married. Pete and Lizzie.*

Pete held out a hand to her. "Climb in, and I'll get our bags."

"Can I fly?"

He kissed her on the cheek and whispered, "No one flies my Jenny but me."

"Is that a yes?"

"You don't know where we're going."

She poked out a pouty bottom lip. "You could tell me."

"Get in front. You can fly us home again."

"I love you so much."

"I love you, too, more than I ever thought possible." He gave her another quick kiss. "Now get in."

She climbed up onto the wing and into the front seat. Pete handed her their bags to put at her feet. He started the aeroplane moving, and she waved to the cheering crowd.

Ivan held Fred and made his paw wave. He'd promised to take care of the dog while they were gone.

Pete thrust the throttle forward, and Jenny took off across the field. Lizzie waited, then felt the rush of leaving the ground. She never grew tired of it. She was flying, and she was married. Two things she had thought would never happen.

The banner fluttered behind them. She turned to try to read it but couldn't. It was enough that she knew what it said. Pete blew her a kiss then flew back and forth across town and even over Wenatchee to let everyone know they were married before heading toward the sunset and their honeymoon.

A Letter To Our Readers

Dear Reader:

In order that we might better contribute to your reading enjoyment, we would appreciate your taking a few minutes to respond to the following questions. We welcome your comments and read each form and letter we receive. When completed, please return to the following:

Fiction Editor
Heartsong Presents
PO Box 719
Uhrichsville, Ohio 44683

1. Did you enjoy reading *Reckless Rogue* by Mary Davis?
   ❑ Very much! I would like to see more books by this author!
   ❑ Moderately. I would have enjoyed it more if

   _____

   _____

   _____

2. Are you a member of **Heartsong Presents**? ❑ Yes ❑ No
   If no, where did you purchase this book? _____

   _____

3. How would you rate, on a scale from 1 (poor) to 5 (superior), the cover design? _____

4. On a scale from 1 (poor) to 10 (superior), please rate the following elements.

   ____ Heroine   ____ Plot
   ____ Hero   ____ Inspirational theme
   ____ Setting   ____ Secondary characters

5. These characters were special because? _____
   _____
   _____

6. How has this book inspired your life? _____
   _____
   _____

7. What settings would you like to see covered in future
   Heartsong Presents books? _____
   _____
   _____

8. What are some inspirational themes you would like to see
   treated in future books? _____
   _____
   _____

9. Would you be interested in reading other **Heartsong
   Presents** titles? ❏ Yes ❏ No

10. Please check your age range:
    ❏ Under 18   ❏ 18-24
    ❏ 25-34   ❏ 35-45
    ❏ 46-55   ❏ Over 55

Name _____

Occupation _____

Address _____

City, State, Zip _____

A BRIDE SO FAIR

Mystery, romance, and intrigue at the Chicago World's Fair. Emily Ralston is delighted when she lands a job at the Children's Building at the fair. When she meets Stephen Bridger, a handsome Colombian Guard, sparks of attraction singe the air. Can Emily and Stephen solve a deadly mystery before time runs out?

Historical, paperback, 288 pages, 5³⁄₁₆" x 8"

Heart**s**ng

HISTORICAL ROMANCE IS CHEAPER BY THE DOZEN!

Any 12 Heartsong Presents titles for only $27.00*

Buy any assortment of twelve *Heartsong Presents* titles and save 25% off of the already discounted price of $2.97 each!

*plus $3.00 shipping and handling per order and sales tax where applicable.
If outside the U.S. please call 740-922-7280 for shipping charges.

HEARTSONG PRESENTS TITLES AVAILABLE NOW:

___HP552 *The Vicar's Daughter*, K. Comeaux
___HP555 *But for Grace*, T. V. Bateman
___HP556 *Red Hills Stranger*, M. G. Chapman
___HP559 *Banjo's New Song*, R. Dow
___HP560 *Heart Appearances*, P. Griffin
___HP563 *Redeemed Hearts*, C. M. Hake
___HP567 *Summer Dream*, M. H. Flinkman
___HP568 *Loveswept*, T. H. Murray
___HP571 *Bayou Fever*, K. Y'Barbo
___HP576 *Letters from the Enemy*, S. M. Warren
___HP579 *Grace*, L. Ford
___HP580 *Land of Promise*, C. Cox
___HP583 *Ramshackle Rose*, C. M. Hake
___HP584 *His Brother's Castoff*, L. N. Dooley
___HP587 *Lilly's Dream*, P. Darty
___HP588 *Torey's Prayer*, T. V. Bateman
___HP591 *Eliza*, M. Colvin
___HP592 *Refining Fire*, C. Cox
___HP599 *Double Deception*, L. Nelson Dooley
___HP600 *The Restoration*, C. M. Hake
___HP603 *A Whale of a Marriage*, D. Hunt
___HP604 *Irene*, L. Ford
___HP607 *Protecting Amy*, S. P. Davis
___HP608 *The Engagement*, K. Comeaux
___HP611 *Faithful Traitor*, J. Stengl
___HP612 *Michaela's Choice*, L. Harris
___HP615 *Gerda's Lawman*, L. N. Dooley
___HP616 *The Lady and the Cad*, T. H. Murray
___HP619 *Everlasting Hope*, T. V. Bateman
___HP620 *Basket of Secrets*, D. Hunt
___HP623 *A Place Called Home*, J. L. Barton
___HP624 *One Chance in a Million*, C. M. Hake
___HP627 *He Loves Me, He Loves Me Not*, R. Druten
___HP628 *Silent Heart*, B. Youree
___HP631 *Second Chance*, T. V. Bateman

___HP632 *Road to Forgiveness*, C. Cox
___HP635 *Hogtied*, L. A. Coleman
___HP636 *Renegade Husband*, D. Mills
___HP639 *Love's Denial*, T. H. Murray
___HP640 *Taking a Chance*, K. E. Hake
___HP643 *Escape to Sanctuary*, M. J. Conner
___HP644 *Making Amends*, J. L. Barton
___HP647 *Remember Me*, K. Comeaux
___HP648 *Last Chance*, C. M. Hake
___HP651 *Against the Tide*, R. Druten
___HP652 *A Love So Tender*, T. V. Batman
___HP655 *The Way Home*, M. Chapman
___HP656 *Pirate's Prize*, L. N. Dooley
___HP659 *Bayou Beginnings*, K. M. Y'Barbo
___HP660 *Hearts Twice Met*, F. Chrisman
___HP663 *Journeys*, T. H. Murray
___HP664 *Chance Adventure*, K. E. Hake
___HP667 *Sagebrush Christmas*, B. L. Etchison
___HP668 *Duel Love*, B. Youree
___HP671 *Sooner or Later*, V. McDonough
___HP672 *Chance of a Lifetime*, K. E. Hake
___HP675 *Bayou Secrets*, K. M. Y'Barbo
___HP676 *Beside Still Waters*, T. V. Bateman
___HP679 *Rose Kelly*, J. Spaeth
___HP680 *Rebecca's Heart*, L. Harris
___HP683 *A Gentlemen's Kiss*, K. Comeaux
___HP684 *Copper Sunrise*, C. Cox
___HP687 *The Ruse*, T. H. Murray
___HP688 *A Handful of Flowers*, C. M. Hake
___HP691 *Bayou Dreams*, K. M. Y'Barbo
___HP692 *The Oregon Escort*, S. P. Davis
___HP695 *Into the Deep*, L. Bliss
___HP696 *Bridal Veil*, C. M. Hake
___HP699 *Bittersweet Remembrance*, G. Fields
___HP700 *Where the River Flows*, I. Brand
___HP703 *Moving the Mountain*, Y. Lehman

(If ordering from this page, please remember to include it with the order form.)

Presents

Great Inspirational Romance at a Great Price!

Heartsong Presents books are inspirational romances in contemporary and historical settings, designed to give you an enjoyable, spirit-lifting reading experience. You can choose wonderfully written titles from some of today's best authors like Wanda E. Brunstetter, Mary Connealy, Susan Page Davis, Cathy Marie Hake, Joyce Livingston, and many others.

When ordering quantities less than twelve, above titles are $2.97 each.
Not all titles may be available at time of order.